undaunted spirit

a westward dreams novel

Books by Jane Peart

Brides of Montclair Series

1 | *Valiant Bride*

2 | *Ransomed Bride*

3 | *Fortune's Bride*

4 | *Folly's Bride*

5 | *Yankee Bride/Rebel Bride*

6 | *Gallant Bride*

7 | *Shadow Bride*

8 | *Destiny's Bride*

9 | *Jubilee Bride*

10 | *Mirror Bride*

11 | *Hero's Bride*

12 | *Senator's Bride*

13 | *Daring Bride*

14 | *Courageous Bride*

Westward Dreams Series

1 | *Runaway Heart*

2 | *Promise of the Valley*

3 | *Where Tomorrow Waits*

4 | *A Distant Dawn*

5 | *Undaunted Spirit*

The American Quilt Series

1 | *The Pattern*

2 | *The Pledge*

3 | *The Promise*

undaunted spirit

a westward dreams novel

BOOK 5

Jane Peart

ZONDERVAN®

ZONDERVAN.com/
AUTHORTRACKER
follow your favorite authors

ZONDERVAN®

Undaunted Spirit
Copyright © 1999 by Jane Peart

Value Edition 978-0-310-28803-9

Requests for information should be addressed to:
Zondervan, *Grand Rapids, Michigan* 49530

Library of Congress Cataloging-in-Publication Data

Peart, Jane.
    Undaunted spirit / Jane Peart.
        p. cm. —(Westward dreams series : bk. 5)
      ISBN 0-310-22012-2
      I. Title. II. Series: Peart, Jane. Westward dreams series ; bk. 5.
  PS3566.E238U54   1999
  813'.54—dc21   99-15208
                                                          CIP

This edition printed on acid-free paper and meets the American National Standards Institute Z39.48 standard.

Interior design by Laura Klynstra

Printed in the United States of America

08 09 10 11 12 13 14 15 16 17 • 18 17 16 15 14 13 12 11 10 9 8 7 6 5 4 3 2 1

undaunted spirit

a westward dreams novel

FOREWORD

"Independence? That's no name for a girl," declared the baby's father.

"Now, Jacob, you named the three boys, and this time it's my turn," came the gentle voice of his wife. "Besides, being born on the Fourth of July must mean something."

"Independence," repeated Grandma Howard, nodding her head as she stitched a pink ribbon onto the flannel receiving blanket.

"It has a pretty sound to it," chimed in Aunt Sassy as she plumped the pillows on her niece's bed. She herself had been named after one of her mother's favorite medicinal herbs, Sassafras.

"Well, if you ask *me,* this family is sure partial to unusual names." Jacob shook his head. But he had long ago given up trying to understand his wife's relatives. After twelve years of marriage, he had accepted the truth of the old saying: You don't just marry the woman, you marry her family. He adored the petite, delicate Percy Howard (her real name was Perseverance), had courted her ardently, married her happily, considered himself lucky to have won her. Her siblings, aunts, uncles, and assorted cousins, however, were another matter, one that often caused him bewilderment if not some irritation, especially their penchant for peculiar names.

Still, Jacob agreed that since his little girl—his first daughter—was born on the country's birthday, she should receive an appropriate name, something symbolic to mark the historic date. He hadn't come up with one to counter his wife's unexpected suggestion, which was seconded by her busybody kin. *Independence.* Jacob's lips formed the word, then his mouth tightened into a straight line. But when he looked at his wife—pale, with lovely blue eyes, dark circled from her ordeal, her lustrous mahogany brown hair braided and fanned out against the ivory pillows—his heart softened. Jacob was always his most vulnerable where Percy was concerned. Whatever she wanted, he wanted her to have.

He straightened his shoulders, "All right, Independence will be her name."

It had been a hectic day. The planned gathering of fifteen of the Howard relatives, invited to celebrate the national holiday, coincided with the baby's arrival, and that had turned everything topsy-turvy. For most of the day the house had been hushed in anticipation of the event, which had come earlier than expected. The other children had been taken to the parade, then to the park for the band concert and picnic. Now, as evening fell, the sound of the fireworks could be heard, and the dark summer sky was alight with sparklers and sky rockets.

From outside came the snap of firecrackers. Aunt Sassy moved quickly to the window. Leaning out she called sharply, "You boys go on away from this side of the house. Your mama and your new little sister need their rest."

Jacob leaned over his wife and kissed her cheek. "I best go down now and leave you to rest." Their eyes met and the mutual love, unspoken, unexpressed, was plain to both of them.

One by one the room emptied. Everyone tiptoed out leaving the mother alone with her baby, the daughter she had hoped for. Percy drew the small bundled infant closer, touched the fluff of red hair covering the tiny, round head, whispered softly, "You're going to have a wonderful life. You have three big brothers who'll love, protect, and take care of you, my little darling."

She lay there, half awake and half asleep, listening to the sounds drifting through the open window and the low murmur of voices and laughter from the front porch where the adults had gathered to eat their strawberry shortcake. Percy smiled to herself. How blessed she was to have a loving family who came in any emergency and took care of things.

Just then, she heard the squeak of the bedroom door being opened carefully, and a minute later a small figure appeared at her bedside. It was four-year-old Farell, her youngest boy. He was small and shy, and he stammered whenever he spoke. He was her "special" child. The other two, Thomas and Ephram, were boisterous, hearty, running, jumping, falling out of trees, climbing fences, shouting, banging in and out of the house with muddy boots, grubby hands, and tousled hair. Farell was quiet and sensitive—and very sweet. He came over to the bed, very close to her, leaned on the coverlet, bent right down into her face, and whispered, "Mama, you all right? Aunt Sassy said—" His voice caught in his throat.

Percy quickly covered his little hand with her own. "I'm fine, darlin', just fine. You're not to worry."

"Aunt Len said you had a hard time, Mama. I was scared."

"Well, there's nothing to be scared about at all. Would you like to see your little sister?"

"Have Tom and Eph seen her?"

"No. You'll be the first," she told him with a soft laugh. She turned back the top of the blanket so he could peek down into the nest she had made of it, and he saw the round, pink face, eyes shut tight. "This is Independence," she introduced them. Percy placed the baby's tiny hand in her brother's saying, "This is your big brother, who's always going to take care of you and protect you, isn't that right, Farell?"

"Yes, Ma'am." He nodded his head vigorously. "What did you name her?"

"Independence."

Farell swallowed. It was a long word. He would have trouble with it, but he tried. "Mmmm-dee—."

"Try it again," his mother urged. "Slowly."

He struggled. "Mmm-dee—."

Percy did not ask him to try again.

And so it happened, as it does sometimes, that the little girl born on the Fourth of July and named Independence would become known within the family, and later in the larger circle of friends and acquaintances, as Mindy—because her brother could not pronounce her name.

PART 1

Chapter 1

Almost from the first, Farell and his younger sister were inseparable. Because Farell constantly got teased at school because of his stuttering, Percy decided to teach him his lessons at home. Mindy, who always wanted to be with her adored brother, sat in on the lessons, and in no time, Percy recognized how bright the little girl was. She had no trouble keeping up with Farell. She was also imaginative and soon began making up little stories, and when she learned her letters, she began writing her stories down in her copy book.

Mindy was far from being a bookworm, however. Even though she preferred the company of the quiet, thoughtful Farell, she was full of energy and had a high-spirited, adventurous personality. Whenever Farell was confined to the house with a cold, Mindy would try to tag along after her two other brothers, who would try to get rid of her by challenging her to perform some hazardous feat. Fiercely competitive, Mindy took any dare until a broken arm, several sprains, bruises, and cuts brought down their father's wrath and their gentle mother's firm reprimand. "You must be kind to your little sister. Remember she's a girl," Percy would admonish while, behind her mother's skirt, Mindy would make faces, stick out her tongue, and waggle her finger at her brothers.

By the time she was ten, Mindy could give as good as she took, and Tom and Eph regarded her warily. Small and wiry, she could outrun them if they took off after her. Fearful of the punishment they might incur if their sister really got hurt, they avoided actual confrontations.

The summer she was twelve things changed. The family had gathered at the McClaren's, as usual, to celebrate the Fourth of July—and, of course, Mindy's birthday. The relatives arrived a few days beforehand from the outlying farms and small towns, and none came empty-handed. Laden with fruits, baked goods, casserole dishes, and delicacies, which were their individual specialties, they came bringing with them an assortment of offspring as well. Mindy and several of her cousins were playing outside in Jacob McClaren's large backyard while the women gathered in the big kitchen. Preparations for the plentiful meal were in full swing. The sound of the egg beater, cream whisker, and batter spoon were heard along with the lively chatter.

Suddenly Aunt Jen gasped, "Law sakes, will you look at that girl?"

"What in the world?" exclaimed Aunt Sassy, joining her at the window.

"My word, now she's hanging by her knees," gasped Grandma Howard, pulling back the starched, checked curtain so she could see better.

"I declare, Percy, you're going to have to do something about that Mindy. She's growing up as wild as a March hare. If you don't watch it, she'll become a regular hoyden."

Jen turned and eyed her niece sternly.

Percy calmly took another stitch in the table runner she was embroidering. "What do you suggest I do?"

"Well, *something*—and *soon*," Jen sounded exasperated. "Certainly, Jacob can."

Percy shook her head slightly. "Mindy's her Papa's pet." She sighed. "He thinks anything she does is either entertaining or amazing."

"If she were *my* daughter—," began Jen, but Sassy interrupted her.

"Well, she isn't, Jen. And we best not offer advice."

Ignoring her sister's rebuke, Jen persisted, "Have you and Jacob discussed sending Mindy to Oakmere Academy? They're known for turning girls into young ladies of refinement."

Again Percy shook her head. "I doubt Jacob would send Mindy away. He'd miss her too much."

"Even for her own good?" Jen frowned. "Maybe, I should talk to Jacob. After all I'm the oldest in our family." Jen's mouth folded into a determined line.

"Please, don't spoil his holiday by getting him all stirred up," Percy begged. "Remember, it's also Mindy's birthday."

"She'll be twelve, won't she? That's time to make plans. After all she'll be sixteen 'fore you know it. Time to think of making a suitable marriage."

"You sure make time fly, Jen," Sassy laughed.

Jen gave her a sharp look. "Well, it's the truth. Before you know it, children are grown up and on their own. If you don't guide them, heavens knows how they'd turn out!"

"'Train up a child in the way he should go and he will not depart from it,'" quoted Sassy.

"Exactly," nodded Jen, unaware of the irony in her sister's tone.

Percy calmly threaded her needle with a strand of red floss and did not comment. She knew her husband. Their only daughter and youngest child was the proverbial "apple of his eye." He would not easily agree to sending her off to boarding school although Oakmere Academy was only thirty miles from Woodhaven and near Philadelphia where many of the Howard relatives had settled.

Endearing pictures of the two of them together passed through her mind. The tall man and the little red-headed girl hand-in-hand when Mindy was first learning to walk, Jacob keeping his long strides short for her tiny steps. Later, Mindy would sit in Jacob's lap while he read to her; later still, with their heads bent over the globe Jacob had bought to show her the world, he would patiently explain to her about oceans, mountains, and plains.

"I want to see all these places!" the little girl would exclaim.

Jacob would assure her, "You can, you *will*, darlin'. You can travel or do anything your li'l heart desires."

He would take her with him when he went fishing. She would trail behind him carrying his creel. Jacob would shoulder his rod and the small fishing pole he made for her. They would spend the whole day together at the river.

No, Percy couldn't imagine Jacob thinking it a good thing for Mindy to go to Oakmere Academy to be made into a proper lady.

The subject was dropped for the moment as one of the husbands strolled into the kitchen and the conversation became general.

But Percy continued to ask herself, Are the aunts right? Was Mindy growing up without manners? True, she did emulate her older brothers in their exploits. She could also be sweet and sensitive and loving with Farell. Mindy instinctively understood how his stammer made him shy and often spoke up for him in difficult situations. Mindy had many good qualities, certainly; she just needed a little polishing, a little decorum. Was Oakmere Academy the right place for her to acquire them?

Percy knew, however, it would take a great deal of persuasion to convince Jacob that this was the correct parental decision for them to make. It was for Mindy's own good, for her future happiness and her ability to make a fine marriage.

"That's a lot of nonsense," was Jacob's first reaction. "She don't need any more schooling. You've said over and over how quick she catches on, how she keeps right up with Farell."

"It's not so much the education, Jacob—it's the atmosphere that'd help her. Here, she's surrounded by her brothers. At Oakmere, there would be girls her own age. She'd learn the basics of grace, how to behave in social situations."

"How to hold a teacup and flutter a fan?" Jacob scoffed.

"It's more than that, Jacob. Being with other girls who are learning ladylike behavior would take off some of the rough edges. Seeing other girls enjoying things like pretty dresses. Learning to dance and play musical instruments could only make Mindy a more attractive person."

"You want her to go?" growled Jacob.

"I'll miss her as much as you will, Jacob. It's not that I *want* her to go; it's that it seems the right thing to do for our daughter."

Jacob always knew when he was overruled. He had an idea the Howard kin had something to do with Percy' suggestion. He never underestimated the influence Percy's family had on her. Besides, what did he know about girls being transformed into young ladies? He'd grown up with brothers and had three sons. Until Mindy was born he didn't know a girl child could nestle in your heart and wind you around her little finger. So he gave in, and Mindy, protesting the whole thirty miles to the school, was enrolled at Oakmere Academy. Her copious tears and dramatic pleading had been to no avail.

Mindy resisted the regimen for the first three weeks, until she finally decided she might as well make the best of it. With her usual optimism, she realized that the sooner she acquired whatever polish she was supposed to get, the sooner she could go home.

She wrote voluminous letters to Farell citing all her complaints about the faculty, her fellow students, the food, and the relentless routine of sewing, piano, deportment—lessons that made up her day. She interjected this report with humorous accounts, character profiles, and incidents that with her keen eye and facile pen made these letters revealing and fun to read.

Mindy enjoyed the poetry classes in particular. She was both exposed to the classics and encouraged to compose her own. Gradually, her own ability to express her thoughts in writing was being honed.

As Aunt Jen had predicted, Mindy's years at Oakmere Academy flew by, and just before her eighteenth birthday, she came home. At first , Mindy simply reveled in being free from all the restrictions she found so odious at Oakmere. She was happy to be with her parents and with Farell again, and she was delighted to receive an invitation to a dancing party at the home of her good friend, Anne Willoughby.

Everyone was struck by the fact that Mindy had been transformed into an attractive, auburn-haired young lady. Outwardly, she had all the manners and grace for which her teachers could take justifiable pride. Inwardly, she had secret hopes and dreams, and a goal unheard of for a woman in 1880.

Chapter 2

The first person Judson Powell noticed when he entered the Willoughbys' house the night of the party was Mindy McClaren. After that, she was the only person he noticed.

She was small and slender and wearing a bright green taffeta dress with a tiered skirt banded with plaid ribbon. Everything about her seemed to shine, her glorious red-gold hair, her eyes, her smile.

Judson, who had overcome his customary reluctance to attend this social function in the first place, asked his host for an introduction. Surprising even Judson, Mindy accepted his request to be his partner for the next dance.

"I don't understand why we've never met before," Judson said as he led her out onto the dance floor.

Mindy tipped her head to look up at her tall partner. A dimple appeared at the corner of her mouth,, "Maybe that's because I've been in prison for the last few years."

"What?" Judson, never quick to pick up on social banter, gasped. At the expression on his face Mindy laughed. Her laughter sounded delightful, and Judson stumbled and lost his step.

"Oakmere Female Academy," Mindy explained, then lowered her voice to a stage whisper, "Can you believe they actually let me out? Not for good behavior, mind you, but because, they were glad to see the last of me."

Judson looked puzzled, his light brown eyebrows drew together over his gray-blue eyes.

"I was a bother, you see," Mindy went on. "Asked too many questions, broke too many rules, was considered a bad influence on the other girls who were trying so hard to turn into proper ladies." Judson managed a smile. It was his first exposure to Mindy's irrepressible sense of humor—and candor. Baffled but enchanted, by the end of the evening he had been completely captured by her charm.

They did not have a chance to become further acquainted, however, because Mindy was soon claimed by the young man to whom she had promised the next dance. To his chagrin, Judson found himself standing on the sidelines the rest of the evening watching Mindy whirl by, dance after dance, with one young man after another, whose names were already written on her dance card.

Still, Judson wasted no time getting his courtship under way. The next morning, a bouquet and a note requesting permission to call arrived at the McClaren house.

Mindy had risen late and was sitting at the kitchen table sipping a cup of tea when her mother brought in the flowers and handed her the small envelope.

"Judson Powell." Mindy read out loud. "Who's he?"

"Just the son of one of the richest men in Woodhaven," replied her mother. "Thomas Powell owns whole mountain sides of timber and the two largest saw mills in the county."

"He says we met at the Willoughbys' last night," Mindy said thoughtfully, dipping her nose into the fragrant mixture of mignonette and lilacs. "But I'm not sure I remember who he is."

In the next few weeks, Judson made sure Mindy could not forget who he was. He became a frequent caller and persistent beau. His intentions were soon clear to everyone except perhaps to Mindy herself.

She was simply enjoying the freedom of being at home again and the privileges rightfully hers as the only daughter in the family. Her two older brothers were both now gone and on their own. Eph had stayed in the army and was presently stationed in Florida. Tom had married his childhood sweetheart, Emily Streeter and was now helping on his father-in-law's farm. Mindy and Farell, the only two still at home quickly resumed their old intimacy. Missing their close relationship had been one of Mindy's trials while away at Oakmere.

Upon returning home, however, Mindy worried about Farell's health. Always delicate since his boyhood bout with diphtheria, Farell seemed thinner and paler than she had remembered, and his wracking cough was a concern.

He dismissed her anxiety, "You're a worrywart. You always dramatize everything. Let's just enjoy the time we have together now."

So they spent the sunny days of that summer at one of their favorite childhood haunts by the river. Taking a picnic basket and books, as well as fishing poles if they were so moved to try their luck, they passed the hours happily. Farell would sometimes read his poetry to her, asking for her comments. Mindy rarely had anything but the highest praise for her beloved brother's work. His words, which he read in his deeply resonant voice, fell like the sweetest music on her ears.

In return, Mindy would read Farell some of her themes she had written at school. Although she had won the literature essay prize upon graduation, she felt somewhat ambivalent about its worth.

"Not that the prize means anything." She made a little face. "The girls who won the embroidery and watercolor painting prizes seemed to get a whole lot more compliments than I did. I suppose it's not considered very ladylike to want to write. Especially to want to be published. And that's what I do want to do, Farell."

"I think it's wonderful, Mindy. There have been some great women writers. Jane Austen, the Brontës, and Harriet Beecher Stowe. Think of the good *she* did with her writing!"

"I don't want to write novels, Farell. I want to write about real things, things that are happening now." She sighed and her lower lip pouted. "There must be more to life than this. I don't intend to spend my life painting China, serving tea to Mama's club ladies, and embroidering pillowcases. That's about all my so-called education at Oakmere fitted me for—" Her blue eyes flashed sparks. "But I had a secret nobody knew about that I worked on all the time I was supposed to be memorizing French verbs." She leaned forward conspiratorially, "Want to hear what it was?"

"Sure," Farell wondered, "What now?" His sister was always up to something.

"I wrote a piece about what I thought was wrong with the way women are educated and sent it to the local newspaper. And guess what—they printed it!"

Farell was impressed. "They did?"

"I sent it in anonymously. Well, not completely. I made up a name. Newspapers have a policy not to print anything signed anonymous. Of course, I couldn't tell anyone I wrote it. It was everything the academy put emphasis on that I didn't agree with. Women's brains are every bit the same as men's. I mean, in scientific studies when they examine two brains, a doctor can't tell which is male, which is female. So why do they think women can't learn the same things as men?"

"I guess because they won't have a chance to use it. Like mathematics, engineering, that sort of thing."

"Well, don't you see, that's exactly what's wrong with the system. If women can learn the same things, why can't they be whatever men can be? Mathematicians, doctors, lawyers, whatever?"

"Ah, Mindy, you would have to change the world to see that happen."

"That's just it. It's unfair. And I don't know what I can do about it."

"Maybe, writing about it *is* the way for you, Mindy. Remember, 'the pen is mightier than the sword.'"

The two always came back from their days by the river together sunburned, exhilarated, and closer than ever. Mindy could bare her heart and soul to no one as completely as she could to Farell.

During the summer, the family would gather on the front porch after supper and visit with friends and neighbors who came by. Of course, there were fewer members now that Eph was away in the army and Tom was newly married to Emily Streeter and living with her parents in the next town. Mindy had missed all this when she was at school. The rhythmic creak of the rockers mingled with the crickets in the grass, and the familiar voices gave her a feeling of security. The soft darkness of the summer evening was broken every so often with the glow of drifting lightning bugs, which lent a certain magic to the scene.

It was almost an intrusion when Judson Powell would stop by. After being offered a seat on one of the white wicker chairs, he would converse politely with Mindy's parents as if that was the sole purpose of his coming. Eventually Percy and Jacob would excuse themselves and leave the porch for the parlor, where Percy would light a lamp as a discreet reminder that Mindy was properly chaperoned. Judson and Mindy would move to the swing at the other end of the porch and sit there talking. Mostly Mindy talked and Judson listened. Mindy had a seemingly endless fund of topics she was interested in discussing.

When Judson attempted to turn their conversation toward something more personal, she would deftly switch the subject. But as summer waned and the first few signs of fall appeared, Judson broached the subject that had long been in his heart, on his mind, and on the tip of his tongue.

One night in early September, he took her hand and held it tight. "Mindy, there's something I must say—I love you. I've loved you since that first evening at the Willoughbys'. I want us to become engaged."

Mindy tugged at her hand, but he wouldn't release it.

"Oh, Judson, I'm not nearly ready to settle down and be married. And that's what being engaged means, after all. I don't want to be married for ages and ages. If ever. I might not want to get married at all."

"You don't mean that!" Judson sounded shocked.

"Yes I do. Very much so."

"But what would you do? I mean, all women want to get married—at least some day."

"Not me. Not necessarily," Mindy said decidedly.

"But I love you."

"Oh, Judson, I know. And I . . . well, I care a great deal for you. But I want to do something with my life. Something different."

"How different?" Judson sounded hurt and puzzled.

"I don't know whether you can understand this or not, Judson," Mindy said slowly.

"Try me," he urged.

"Well, I want to write. Not just verses or little stories, but important things. Writing that will change things."

"What sort of things?"

"I can't say precisely *what*. There are any number of things I feel so strongly about that if I could just write about them, then maybe I could persuade people to feel the same way."

"Why couldn't you do that and be married too?"

Mindy sighed. "Maybe you could. Maybe *someone* could. I'm not sure *I* could, Judson. When I'm doing something

I'm really interested in I forget about everything else. Just ask my mother. For example, just the other day she had a whole pot of plums simmering on the stove getting ready to make jam. She asked me to watch it and stir it every fifteen minutes so that they wouldn't burn or boil over. Then she left for a few minutes. I was bored with the task, if you want to know the truth. So I went back to the book I was reading, holding it in one hand while I held the spoon with the other. Well, you can guess what happened. Before I knew it, the pot boiled over and all this sticky, gooey purple stuff began to pour out of the pot all over the stove, the floor . . . so you see, Judson, in the kitchen I'm hopeless."

Judson laughed at Mindy's lack of culinary skill, then he said, almost shyly, "I'm sure you don't know this, Mindy, but my family is, well, maybe not rich, but pretty well off. If you married me, you wouldn't have to watch plums boiling or anything like that. You'd have a hired girl to do that sort of thing. A maid too, like my mother has. I want that for you. I want you to do what you want. I want you to be happy, Mindy. And I promise you, I'd do everything to make sure you were happy."

Mindy looked at his handsome face, his earnest expression. She knew he believed everything he was saying. Her heart softened, melting some of the clarity in her mind and some of the decisiveness of her words. Maybe, with Judson, it could work out. He was sweet, kind, and he certainly loved her. But would she be giving up something important if she said yes? Would she be giving up that core of herself that was as unique and individual as her name—Independence?

Chapter 3

*I*n spite of Judson's flattering attention, the comfort of being at home, and the pleasure of Farell's companionship, Mindy was restless. The days began to seem long and pointless, and she longed for something worthwhile to do. It was well enough to vent her frustrations to the understanding Farell, still, nothing would happen if she didn't take action.

After some agitated inner debate, Mindy came to a decision. Nothing ventured, nothing gained. What good did it do to complain about the way things are? Why not try to change them?

Mindy surveyed herself in her bedroom mirror, dressed to embark on a bold venture. Did she look like someone who should be taken seriously? Her biscuit-tan linen skirt, tucked bodice, and nipped-in jacket was suitably sensible, she decided. She secured her straw hat firmly with a hatpin, picked up the portfolio containing some of her best essays, plus the two letters-to-the-editor she had written and published.

She opened her bedroom door quietly and peered into the hall. She tiptoed past her mother's bedroom, where

Percy was taking a nap, and down the stairs, and out of the house. She walked downtown and, before she lost her nerve, straight to the office of the *Woodhaven Courier Journal.*

Once inside the entrance, Mindy asked a man behind a counter—under a sign reading INFORMATIONwhere the newsroom was.

"Down the hall and to your right," he said without looking up from his newspaper.

Following his directions Mindy found herself at the door of a long room in which there were several desks. The men who were seated at them did not look busy. One had his feet up; two others, to her amazement, were playing cards; and two others were standing at a water cooler.

At the very back she saw a desk with a small wooden plaque on it. ED JAMISON, EDITOR. That must be who she should talk to about getting a job, she decided, She headed in that direction. As she passed by on her way, one man looked up from the paper he had spread out on his desk top, and Mindy noticed he was working a crossword puzzle. What kind of a newspaper was this?

Upon reaching the editor's desk, Mindy said, "Good afternoon, Mr. Jamison."

The man pushed back the green eye-shade he was wearing and surveyed her. Through thick glasses, his eyes met an unusual sight in the clutter and muddle of his newsroom: a pretty young woman, fashionably dressed in a tan silk suit, banded with brown braid, wearing gloves and a perky straw hat trimmed with taffeta bows. Had she stumbled into the wrong place? He regarded her for a few seconds; "If you're looking to place an ad, miss, classified will help you."

Trying not to let her voice shake, Mindy said, "No, sir, I don't want to place an ad. I want a job." ."A job?"

"Yes."

"What kind of a job?" He looked annoyed. "Doing what?"

"Reporting," she replied. "I want a job as a reporter."

"A reporter?" His jaw literally dropped. He shook his head. "I don't need a reporter. I've got all the reporters I need."

"They don't look very busy. Aren't there stories out there that need to be covered?"

"You've got a sharp tongue, young lady," he said gruffly. "For your information they're waiting for a jury to reach a verdict over at the courthouse. They've been out for nearly three hours. That's what they're doin'. When they get the word the jury is ready to deliver its verdict and court is reconvened, they'll be over there in a flash. After that, this newsroom'll be a beehive. Does that answer your question?"

"In the meantime, who's covering whatever else may be happening?"

Jamison looked at her, a flicker of interest in his eyes.

Mindy acted on her advantage and held out her portfolio. "Here is some published work of mine. You can see for yourself that I'm qualified." He took the portfolio with a skeptical look and opened it. Turning the pages, he stopped every once in awhile to read a passage here and there. He looked up at her again.

"These are signed by Howard McClaren."

"I used that name because I thought something written by a male would receive more attention, more respect than one by a woman," Mindy said firmly. "But they *are* mine. My thoughts, feelings, and opinions."

Jamison still seemed to need reassurance. "You wrote all these? Yourself?"

"Yes, Sir," Mindy replied, a spark of hope springing up. After a long moment, Jamison said slowly, "Well, you can write, I can see that. Know how to spell and how to punctuate."

Jamison reached for a batch of papers in his wire IN basket. "Maybe, this is something you could do, the advice column. It's been written by a minister over in Danville, but he's retiring or going to Africa to preach to the heathens or something, although he'd probably be better off staying right here, plenty of heathens to convert around here!" He gave a short laugh. "Anyway, he's given up the job. But there're people, readers who keep writing letters asking for help . . ." He paused. "Want to tackle it?"

For a moment, Mindy was stunned. Of course she knew the "Dixie Dillon" column. Everybody did. She sometimes read it, giggled over it, had always taken it lightly. That people actually wrote in asking for advice on their most personal problems had always seemed strange to her. Now she was being offered to write the column herself.

To take over a job held by a minister of the gospel, to give advice about problems she'd probably never experienced or, for that matter, had never even thought of—was she up to that kind of challenge? Then she remembered how the girls at school had begged her to help them write their love letters. She had been pretty good at it, even if she said so herself.

"Well?" demanded Jamison.

"Well, it wasn't exactly what I had in mind—" She hesitated.

"Take it or leave it." He shrugged and started to replace the pile of papers.

"No, wait, I'll take it."

With a great show of reluctance, Jamison stuffed the letters into a large manila envelope and handed it to her.

"Do three sample columns and bring 'em in. Then we'll see."

At just that moment the newsroom door burst open and a skinny little boy ran in shouting, "Jury's reached a verdict—the judge's been sent for!"

There was an immediate scramble as reporters got to their feet, grabbed jackets and notebooks, and rushed out. One, who seemed to be taking his time, commented languidly,

"No need to hurry. First, they'll have to pry Judge Hurley out of the Pig 'n Whistle." Mindy knew he was referring to a local tavern near the courthouse.

Mindy stood in the now emptied newsroom, clutching the envelope of letters. Inside it were pitiful tales of heartbreak, trials, troubles of all sorts, of which she herself was ignorant. Could she fill the gap left by a man of the cloth with years of dealing with such things? Whatever her misgivings, she knew this was her chance, her opening into a world she was eager to enter.

Chapter 4

*A*ccident at the corner of Mason and Conway!" came the shout.

Mindy, at her desk, shoved into a cubbyhole of the newsroom, looked up from the pile of letters she was sorting through for the next day's "Dixie Dillon" column.

Two reporters, who had been working at their desks, pushed back their chairs and hurried out. Mindy went back to working on her column, feeling a bit resentful. There was no reason why she couldn't cover a story as well as any of the male reporters.

She had proved herself with the assignment Jamison had given her. They were getting more letters than ever for the column. Maybe she couldn't quote Scripture as well as the Reverend Downing had, but she gave practical, down-to-earth advice that people seemed to welcome and appreciate.

Of course, it was all still her secret. She hadn't told anyone but Farell that she was now "Dixie Dillon." It was their private joke. She often shared some of the letters with him, asking for his viewpoint and believing that his masculine input gave the column a better balance. Since she only went in two days a week for a few hours, her parents thought she was doing clerical work for the newspaper.

At first she had avoided telling Judson the exact nature of her job. She told him she was answering letters to the paper.

"You're a secretary to the editor?"

"Not exactly," she hedged. Then knowing it would have to come out sooner or later, she told him the truth. His reaction was exactly what she thought it would be.

"That's the most ridiculous thing I ever heard of, and besides it's dishonest. Those people really believe Dixie Dillon is a wise, old lady with all the answers. How can you pretend something like that?"

But whether Judson approved or not, Mindy was determined to keep the assignment in the hope that it would eventually lead to a real reporter's job.

Sadly, Mindy had already decided that Judson had neither much imagination nor a sense of humor. To him things were clear cut, black or white. Still, he had other good qualities.

Resignedly, Mindy turned back to her work. She selected a letter and began to read:

Dear Dixie Dillon,

My sister is my problem. Every time my boyfriend comes to call, she comes wherever we are, in the parlor, on the porch, out in the side yard and plunks herself right there, won't budge, until finally he gives up and leaves. How can I get her to understand we might want some privacy. (That is without her going running to Mama and telling tales?)
Signed,
Frustrated

Dear Frustrated,

Are you sure you want to be alone with your caller? You didn't say whether your sister was younger or older than you. If she's older, maybe your sister's protecting you from unwanted advances or maybe she's interested in your caller herself?

If she is younger, there may be ways to entice her to go somewhere else when your friend calls.

Mindy sighed and mentally tried a different approach. Then she put that letter aside. She decided it wouldn't make a very interesting one on which to base her column anyway. She picked up the next one.

Dear Dixie Dillon:

My husband spends most of his pay on drink. Unless I meet him at the factory gate on Friday he goes to the saloon with his buddies, and the children and I go without food. We're behind with the rent and coal bill.

This kind of letter came frequently and infuriated Mindy. These poor women probably had married with the idea they were going to be protected and provided for, and now they lived dismal lives. They awakened in her a real fear of ever being dependent on a man.

This attitude did not do much to help Judson Powell's chances. The more he begged Mindy to accept his ring, the more she resisted. "You don't have work at that grubby paper," he would complain when she made the excuse that she had her column to write when he wanted to take her for a ride in his new buggy. He was as jealous of her job as he would be of another suitor. What Judson wanted to see in that newspaper was the announcement of their engagement!

"Give me six months, Judson. Then we'll talk about marriage. I feel sure Mr. Jamison is going to give me the opportunity to report a real news story soon."

Mindy wasn't as sure of that as she pretended. In fact, her last discussion with her editor on just that point had been discouraging. She had been working at the newspaper for nearly three months. Being Dixie Dillon provided some outlet for her creative energy—but not enough. She longed to do some of the stories the men reporters were doing. She felt she could write just as well—even better than some of them. In her opinion, they often left out the very things that she felt were the most important, things that readers would be interested in knowing. Although they usually followed the reportorial credo of "what, where, when, who, how," it seemed to Mindy that they often skipped the "who," the human side. They could do a fine job recounting the facts of a trial, but what about the family of the convicted man? What about the wife and children of someone being sent off to prison? They had a story to tell too. But no one was telling it. In those reports of accidents, burglaries, decisions of the city council—there were always human beings behind the headlines, ordinary people caught in extraordinary circumstances. Mindy longed to delve into those stories.

However, when she approached Mr. Jamison begging for a chance to attend a trial, interview a relative, or report on an accident, his dismissing answer was always, "One of the men is covering that."

"Why can't I try a real news story?"

"You're not a full-time reporter, for one thing."

"Let me do one story, then see—"

"I've got plenty of reporters to cover everything that happens in Woodhaven. Stick to your Dixie Dillon column. You're doing a great job there. Good stuff."

"I can do as good a job as any reporter if I had a chance."

He looked up at her, an annoyed frown on his face. "I'm sure you could, but then I'd have to pay you a reporter's wages."

"Well, why not?"

"You're a single young woman for one reason. Most of the reporters are supporting a family on their salaries."

Mindy sighed and kept threading through her mail doggedly searching for one that would make a compelling story on which she could tag an eye-catching headline.

"McClaren!" a loud voice called, jolting Mindy out of her absorption. "You better come. Now!"

She looked up and saw Jeff Singleton, one of the reporters, his face ashen, eyes wide standing at the door of the newsroom, motioning to her wildly. Alarm streaked through her. She stumbled to her feet, scattering the papers and letters off her desk to the floor. Automatically she reached for her hat, jammed it on her head and hurried through the web of desks toward him. He grabbed her arm and pulled her along with him, down the steps of the newspaper building, out onto the street and along the sidewalk. Ahead of them a circle of people was gathered three deep. Mindy heard a police whistle and saw two uniformed officers trying to push back the crowd.

"Press!" shouted Jeff. "Let us through."

The shrill jangle of an ambulance siren cut through the air, as Jeff shoved her forward and she elbowed her way through. A blur of faces turned toward her. Later she remember they were faces of people she knew and from their look of shocked recognition, who also knew her.

Outside, several men were attempting to lead two terrified horses, wild-eyed and snorting with fear, away from where the two vehicles had collided. One was a wagon loaded with haystacks; the other a light buggy. Reaching the edge of the crowd, Mindy stopped. A scream rose, then caught in her throat, and she clutched it with both hands.

The man lying on the road, blood streaming from a gash on his forehead, was her father, Jacob McClaren. He lay white and motionless, his usually immaculate white linen shirt stained crimson. As Mindy stood frozen, she heard someone say, "Here comes Dr. Semple, make way." She couldn't speak or move. All she could do was watch in helpless agony as the doctor bent over the prone body of her beloved father. Then, unbelieving, she heard him say, "It's no use. He's gone."

The next few days Mindy moved in shadows. Her doting, adored father was dead. His death was so shockingly sudden. Nothing could have prepared her for it. It wasn't as though he had been in failing health or enduring a long illness. Jacob McClaren was at the peak of his health, a young, hearty man in his early forties. What was hardest of all for Mindy to bear was that she had no chance to say good-bye. She couldn't even remember anything much about their last morning together. At the breakfast table, her mind had been too preoccupied about the day ahead at the newspaper, so distracted she could not even recall what they had talked about. She deeply regretted how absent-mindedly she had turned her cheek for his kiss as her father had left for the hardware store. Oh, if only she had a chance to relive that hour. She would have jumped up from the table, run to hug him at the front door before he went down the porch steps and climbed into his buggy. If somehow we realized any parting could be a last.

Dazed with grief, Mindy saw everything as through a veil of unreality. Neighbors came with covered dishes and pies, friends called, relatives arrived. The funeral, the flowers, the reception after the graveside ceremony—all passed before her as though in some kind of dream, a dream she didn't want, from which she desperately wished she could awaken.

Then came the aftermath, the chilling information that Jacob had left nothing for his widow. The McClaren Hardware Store had seemed prosperous enough. But the very qualities of Jacob's that had been so highly eulogized at his burial service—his generosity and kindness—were now the stark realities of his family's situation. There was no money.

Through her tears, Percy repeated over and over, "He was the most generous man I ever knew, so free-handed, he'd loan money to anyone who asked and never ask repayment. When I'd sometimes suggest that the recipient was unworthy, Jacob would just smile and say, 'The Lord keeps the books. Not for us to judge, give with an open heart.'"

Now the day of reckoning had come. The three dollars a week Mindy earned at the newspaper could no longer be frittered away on bonnet ribbons or books; instead, it had to be turned over to her mother for groceries.

There was no one else on whom Percy could depend. After the funeral, Mindy's brother Ephram returned to his army post in Florida. Tom and his wife, Emily, lived in the next town, where they were building a house on her family's farm and expecting their first baby. Farell's health continued to be poor, and because of it, he could not hold a job. So it was up to Mindy to be the breadwinner. She must make more money. Somehow, she decided, she must become a full-time reporter for the newspaper. The question was: *How?* No sooner had she determined to present her case with renewed insistence to Jamison than a new problem surfaced.

After their father's death, Farell's health began deteriorating even more rapidly. One terrible night Mindy and her mother kept vigil by Farell's bedside, trying to ease his wracking cough. Dr. Semple was called. When he examined Farell, the doctor looked grave.

"I hate to tell you this Mrs. McClaren, but this young man has incipient tuberculosis. If you don't get him to a milder climate, see that he has plenty of rest, nourishing food, fresh air . . ." He shook his head, "Unless he does, I can't say that he even has a year to live."

Stunned, Mindy and her mother were at a loss. Where could they send Farell? Fortunately, Dr. Semple, a longtime friend as well as their family physician, told Percy he had relatives in North Carolina in the mountain area noted for its climate's restorative benefits for consumptives. He would make arrangements for Percy and Farell to go there at once. They could board with the Asbury family, who accommodated such patients. Without delay, this was arranged. Mindy was to stay in Woodhaven until Farell recovered sufficiently to return.

While they were gone, the McClaren's family home was to be put up for sale, and Mindy was to stay with Aunt Jen. Since the arrangement was temporary, Mindy didn't mind the fact that it was into her aunt's sewing room she moved. Other decisions could be delayed. The money from the sale of the house would provide Percy with living expenses for quite a few years.

Mindy's heart wrenched in parting from her loved ones. Since her father's death, she had relied more and more on Farell. In spite of his frail health, he was strong in heart and spirit, with a deep religious faith that sustained her. Each tried to put on a brave face, but not knowing how long the separation would be made their parting harder.

Chapter 5

The day Mindy put her mother and Farell on the train for North Carolina she stood on the platform, looking after the train as it steamed down the tracks and finally disappeared. The image of her mother's face, framed in her crêpe-draped widow's bonnet, made her heart ache, and the already weary expression on Farell's pale face was etched in her memory. Mindy wondered whether she might not be seeing her adored brother for the last time.

Disconsolately, Mindy walked back to the office. On her desk awaited a pile of letters, which had arrived in the morning mail. The volume of mail for Dixie Dillon had grown with each succeeding week. Today, she did not feel her usual anticipation about opening them or the creative energy to answer them. She felt empty inside, with no answers for anyone—not even herself. She felt cut loose from her moorings. Everything she thought of as permanent was gone. Staying with Aunt Jen did not appeal to her even though she knew it was temporary. Until her mother and brother returned or, as everyone assumed—especially

Judson—that when the proper period of mourning had been observed, she would get married.

Mindy still wanted to become a bona fide reporter before settling down to a life of "domestic bliss." This remained a source of many arguments between Judson and her—arguments that were never settled. Mindy wished he understood her need. But maybe that was asking too much.

To distract herself, Mindy settled down to work. Half-heartedly, she pulled out the first letter from the stack and began to read it. Just then from down the street came the familiar shrill sound of the fire alarm whistle. A few minutes later the rattle and roar of the horse-drawn fire engine clattered past the newspaper office. Mindy looked up as a couple of the reporters rushed out to follow the fire engine to the scene.

Mindy sighed and went doggedly back to work. She would have liked to be sent out on an assignment with some excitement, some drama, some human interest. But of course, covering fires was not considered her "beat." She was relegated to the Women's Page, articles covering the activities of the Garden Club, recipes from church suppers and social events of various kinds—things in which she herself had no interest. Not only did she detest attending such events, she liked writing about them even less. How could she convince Mr. Jamison that she was capable of serious reporting?

Forty-five minutes later, the two reporters returned, and Mindy overheard some of the details of the fire. A boarding house had been razed. A grease spill on the stove ignited it, and soon the whole building had gone up in flames like a tinderbox. Flimsy construction, no fire escapes, no kitchen pump from which water could have been drawn to put it out right away. "The whole place was a disaster waiting to happen," remarked one of the men as he took off his coat and sat down at his desk to write his report.

As the two reporters discussed the fire, Mindy could not help but overhear. The boarders, they said, were mostly girls from the local shoe factory. Mindy had received letters from some of these workers, for they would often pour out their hearts to Dixie Dillon about their troubles: boyfriends, family quarrels, squabbles with a co-worker, working conditions. Their lives seemed drab enough without suffering a loss like this.

What struck Mindy was that the two men didn't mention the girls themselves, who were at work when it happened but were now without a place to live. Hadn't anyone interviewed them? Who told them their living quarters had been destroyed? The factory managers? Or had they just let them go on working while the fire consumed all their belongings? Did their employers just let them find out when the whistle blew at the end of the workday? The heartlessness of the situation touched Mindy's tender heart. Where would they go to find a place to live or even spend this night? Did anyone know? Did anyone care?

Mindy had a hard time sleeping that night. Not only did she miss her mother and Farell, but she couldn't get those homeless factory girls off her mind. How could she help?

A few days later, in her mail, Mindy found out. A letter gave her the clue . It was from a girl named Aggie Sloane, a factory worker, left homeless by the boarding house fire. Written on rough, lined paper in a poor childish handwriting, it came straight from the heart.

Not that it was much of a place anyway. Some would call it a rabbit's warren, four of us cramped into one small room. We shared a bureau and each had a chair and the bathroom was down two floors. But even so, it were our own. And most of us was friends and got along fine. Now, we're scattered all over town anywheres we could find a room and some are pretty awful. Want half of what our weekly wages is. Most

41

get breakfast but no evening meal. But you gotta take whatever you can. I'd chuck it all and go back home if I had one to go to, but Ma's married again and there's lots of little ones now. I ain't a complainer usually. But what's a girl to do?

That plaintive question rang in Mindy's ears. It also gave her an idea. She would combine the letter with the reports of the fire and present the victim's dilemma in an article that Jamison would be compelled to print. It would give her a chance to show her writing ability along with presenting the real problem of this girl and others like her. The devastating fire was not just a dramatic news report but a human tragedy. Dixie Dillon's reply would follow the letter. It would be an answer designed to touch people's hearts. She would show that these girls needed more than a decent place to live that they could afford, but also some comfort, some fun, some joy.

Mindy put aside the other letters and concentrated on writing a response to Aggie Sloane's question. She worked steadily all afternoon, writing, rewriting, scratching out, tearing up, starting over again. Into the piece she poured some of her own emotions of being without a family, a real home, her lack of security and fear of the future.

When Mr. Jamison returned from the city council meeting, he gave her a curious look as he passed by on his way to his own desk, but he made no comment.

At last satisfied with the finished article, she copied it out carefully, attached it to Aggie's letter, then walked over to Mr. Jamison's desk. She stood there a full minute before he looked up. Then she placed it on top of his pile of copy to be okayed.

"Please read this, Mr. Jamison."

He gave her an irritated look, mumbled something about being overworked as it was. Mindy said, "Please, Mr. Jamison."

"Oh, all right." He picked it up and she watched as his eyes moved rapidly across the page. Then he seemed to slow down and his reading became more deliberate. Finally he looked up at her. "This is good."

"Really?" Mindy let out the breath she had been holding.

He took his pen and scrawled a huge "OK" on it, then handed it back to her. The copy boy had already left for the day, so Mindy took it into the composing room herself and left it with the compositor to be set in the Dixie Dillon column for the next day's edition.

The following afternoon, fresh off the press and still smelling of newly printed ink, that day's edition was placed on Mindy's desk by the mail clerk. With trembling hands Mindy opened it to the page where the Dixie Dillon column appeared and saw in bold type "WHAT'S A GIRL TO DO?"

Mindy read it through twice, relishing her choice of words and feeling a lump rise in her throat,

What if your own daughter were out in the world alone trying to make her way, working from six in the morning to six in the evening, and then had no place warm, comfortable, and welcoming to go to? We all benefit from the product these factory girls make as they stand at their machines hour after hour, so shouldn't we do something to make their lives happier, safer, pleasanter? Shouldn't we provide a place where they can gather to socialize, read, have refreshments? Would that not eliminate the harmful and often dangerous practice some of these lonely girls fall into of taking up with strange men, going with them to a tavern or worse, risking their virtue and even their very lives? We owe it to these girls who could be our sisters, our daughters, to do whatever we can.

She saw a few things in it she might, given the chance, change, a word that might have been better used. On the whole she was proud of the column. For the first time, it seemed really hers, not just something she had taken over from someone else. Before, she had adhered as much as possible to what her predecessor, the minister, had done, copying his style and the language of his replies. But today, the column had heart. It was *hers*. *She* felt she *was* truly Dixie Dillon.

Later that evening, when Judson came over to the house, she asked him, "So what do you think?"

"It's a fine article, Mindy," he acknowledged. "But I'd rather talk about us. Mother keeps asking when we're going to announce our engagement. She wants to give a party for us."

"Well, it would hardly be appropriate, Judson. My father's only been dead a few months. I'm still officially in mourning."

"I realize that, honey," Judson said, taking her hand. "But now with your mother and Farell gone, it isn't right for you to be alone. I want to take care of you. I want us to get married, Mindy."

Gently, Mindy withdrew her hand. "You said you'd give me time, Judson. I think Mr. Jamison is coming around. I think he's considering giving me reporter status."

"Ah, Mindy!" Judson exclaimed exasperated. He got up from the swing where they'd been sitting. He plunged his hands in his pockets, walked over to the edge of the porch, and stood at the railing. Mindy could tell by the set of his shoulders that he was angry. "I'm afraid you'll just keep putting it off. There'll always be some reason, some excuse. Why is that stupid job more important than us?"

"It isn't a stupid job, Judson, and of course, it's not more important than us," she protested. "Can't you understand that I want to accomplish something on my own before I settle down and become just a housewife."

"You'd not be 'just a housewife,' as you call it. And plenty of girls would be happy to be that, by the way.

Mother thinks—" He halted, biting his lower lip as if he realized that his mother's opinion might not be the most diplomatic thing to quote to Mindy at this point.

What Mrs. Powell had actually said was, "What's the matter with that girl? Any girl in this town would be thrilled to have a young, handsome, personable man like you in love with her, begging her to get married. I think she's foolish and headstrong, and my advice to you, Son, is to give some long and serious thought about pursuing this relationship any further."

"I love Mindy, Mother. And I *am* going to marry her. No matter what," Judson had said adamantly.

It was the "no matter what" that Judson was struggling with now.

Mindy came over to where he stood and put a tentative hand on his coat sleeve. "Don't be cross, Judson. Be happy for me. Having this article printed without Mr. Jamison blue-penciling a single word or cutting it was really quite a step. You don't know how much that means."

Judson became aware of her nearness, the scent of apple blossoms on her hair and skin. His irritation faded away. He turned around and took Mindy in his arms, felt the warmth of her small, slender body under the crisp cotton blouse. He bent to kiss the warm, soft sweetness of her lips. He knew he couldn't give Mindy up. No matter what his mother thought. Sure she was independent, outspoken and, yes, stubborn. Still, no matter how long it took he was determined to have her. She had spoiled any other girl for him.

Chapter 6

$\mathscr{T}$he response to "What's a Girl to Do?" was greater than Mindy could have imagined. Mail began to pour into the newspaper office, first a trickle, then a flood. Mindy's prose had touched even the hardest hearts in town with her question, "What if it were your daughter, or sister, alone in the world, forced to fend for herself?"

All sorts of suggestions and offers came as a result of Aggie Sloane's letter, which Mindy had enhanced, adding details but written in the ungrammatical prose of the original. Mindy had somehow stepped into the girl's place, told her story with poignancy appealing to the best in human nature.

Church Ladies United held a special meeting to see what they could do to better the factory girls' lives. One of the local churches voted to keep their parish hall open in the evenings providing a place for the girls to gather after working hours. When this was announced, others entered into the plan. A lending library of wholesome books was started, a sewing center with a sewing machine and supplies was organized with volunteers to help the girls and teach them, refreshments of apple cider and homemade cookies and pies were donated. Everyone rallied around to show kindness to a group that had been largely ignored. Unusual friendships were formed between the factory girls and the women of the town who had been indifferent to each other before.

"Well, looks like you've done it, little lady." Mr. Jamison stopped by her desk and tapped his forefinger on the stacks of letters that covered it. "Got enough work to do? Letters to answer?"

Mindy had learned that underneath Jamison's gruff manner was a tender-hearted man easily moved by emotion. She had been sure once he read her article about Aggie Sloane he would allow her to print it.

"Yes, sir." Mindy replied. Although slightly overwhelmed by the response, the problem was everyone thought it was *Dixie Dillon's* triumph not hers. *What was the use of writing such a successful piece if no one knew it was yours?* She asked herself with some chagrin.

"Well, keep up the good work," Jamison said and went back to his own desk.

Keep up the good work? Mindy raised her eyebrows. What did that mean? That she was stuck forever here as the advisor to the lovelorn? Even after what had happened as a result of "What's a Girl to Do?"

No, she realized. She would somehow have to top even that if she were to move ahead. At least now she knew she could step into someone else's life and write from their viewpoint. The possibilities were unlimited. She would just have to cull her mail, pick out an equally compelling problem, and dramatize it. In her heart, Mindy knew she had a gift, and she meant to use it.

Letters from readers continued to flow onto the desk of Dixie Dillon. It was, however, a letter from her mother that temporarily took her mind off her journalistic career. It was of a far more personal nature. Percy had written regularly ever since she and Farell had arrived in North Carolina. Descriptions of the Asbury's lovely home, the mild climate, and their gracious host were described in detail. Mindy had kept her mother's first letter to reread often to reassure herself that they had made the right decision.

> Dr. Semple could not have prescribed a more pleasant or peaceful place for your brother to find rest and recovery. Farell was quite worn out when we arrived, however. We were met at the train by Mr. Belvedere Asbury, who as you may recall, was a college classmate of Dr. Semple. They have remained friends all these many years. Mr. Asbury is the epitome of a southern gentleman. He is very tall, dressed in a gray linen suit and an immaculate white shirt with a black bow string tie. His features are noble, his hair thick, wavy and silver-gray, his manners . . . well, think of a lord at some court. He welcomed us in a soft, slow voice, saw to our luggage and put us in his surrey with great courtesy.
>
> The house, called "Linden Hill" set back from a country road in a grove of sweeping pine trees, is white, the windows framed by dark green shutters, and a deep porch leads through a fan-lighted door into the cool interior. His sister, Miss Louella, is as gentle and dainty as one could imagine, dressed in fluttery ruffles, and she speaks in a low and musical voice.
>
> They made us feel immediately at home. I know in this environment, Farell is going to begin to feel better every day. For myself, I thank the good Lord for the friendship that brought us here and I am eternally grateful.

The six weeks that Dr. Semple had suggested would be needed for Farell to show any improvement lengthened. Two months later Percy wrote,

> Each time I suggest to the Asburys that perhaps we better make plans to leave, they both urge us to remain, offering all sorts of enticements. There is to be a special party, or they are planning a day trip to see Chimney Rock, or a neighbor is giving a picnic in our

honor. This climate has been so beneficial to Farell that I dare not refuse to stay longer. The Asburys are very persuasive, I wish you knew this lovely family as we have come to know them.

Each successive letter from Percy extolled the Asbury brother and sister. It seemed there was no end to their thoughtfulness. Each letter added another incident showing some further gesture of their kindness to both the McClarens. There were mentions of Mr. Asbury's taking Percy for rides in the country, of introductions to equally genteel neighbors, of Miss Louella's interest in Farell's poetry, in fact, her setting one of his poems to music. It seemed Louella was quite talented at the piano and often gave concerts at social evenings. There were other accounts of afternoon teas and even dinner parties given by friends of the Asburys, at which Percy and Farell were honored guests.

Mindy wasn't sure at what point and in which letter her mother had started to call Mr. Asbury by his first name, Belvedere. Even so, upon opening her mother's letter this particular day, Mindy had not the slightest premonition of what it contained.

It had been nearly six months since her father's death and five since her mother and Farell had left for North Carolina. The large McClaren house had not as yet sold. Realtors said it needed repairs and remodeling, which had been largely done piecemeal over the years of the family's occupancy. To a prospective buyer these things became points over which to quibble for lowering the asking price. Mindy felt a vague uneasiness about all this. While she stayed busy with her work and spent most evenings with Judson, she tried to ignore the misgivings about the eventual sale of the house. Somewhere in the back of her mind was the unrealistic hope that her mother and Farell would return, and they could all move happily back into the family home.

She was totally unprepared for the drastic changes that she had not foreseen. She slit open the envelope and took out three thin pages of stationery written in her mother's fine penmanship. "I hope it is not going to come as too much of a shock," it began,

to tell you that Belvedere has asked me to be his wife. I have come to know, admire, and respect him very much in the time I have been here. He is the perfect gentleman, a wonderful companion, and I believe will be a wonderful husband. He was married once but was widowed after only three months. He told me that until now, no woman could possibly have replaced his bride. Not that I would ever want to erase the memory of the lovely young person he married at twenty, but I take it as a great compliment that such a refined, intelligent, interesting man wants to marry me.

After your dear father died I never thought to love again nor to remarry. That I should again have the love of a fine man for a second time in my life did not even seem possible. But this has happened, and I accept it gratefully.

A life without someone to whom you are special can be a lonely one, without purpose or joy. This, my dear daughter, is what I know you have in full measure with Judson. If I wasn't assured how much Judson cares for you, wants to protect and provide for you, I would never consider Belvedere's proposal. But knowing you and Judson will soon marry makes this decision easier for me. I hope you understand.

Farell does so heartily. He has come to regard Belvedere as a dear friend and, moreover, as an older brother. His health has improved almost miraculously since we came, and the doctors here feel he may soon be completely restored to health. He and Louella have become fast friends, they work on putting Farell's poems to music nearly every day and enjoy each other's company immensely.

I told Belvedere I wanted to write to my daughter and get her approval and blessing before we announce our plans formally.

Approval?

Was her mother really asking her for advice? A smile tipped the corners of Mindy's mouth. Shades of Dixie Dillon. Her own mother writing to "lovelorn columnist?" It was almost funny. Actually, it seemed Percy had already made up her mind. Percy closed the letter by saying,

I have also written the bank and instructed them to take whatever offer they receive on our house. I see no reason to hold out for more money. Belvedere has assured me I never need worry about financial matters. He also joins me in love to you and the hope that one day soon you may decide to come here and make your home. He says you would be most welcome.

Did her mother really think she would give up her job and go to live with the Asburys in North Carolina? Her mother must be completely dazzled by her new romance to think that she would. From the letters, Mindy envisioned the picture of the happy foursome at the Asbury's country home. There was no place there for her even if she wanted to go.

She was happy for her mother and brother. The tiny nagging sensation of being left out was only momentary. She had her own life to live, and, of course, there was Judson.

Mindy refolded the letter and put it back in the envelope. After this startling news, Mindy knew she must make plans of her own. She knew that once she told Judson of her mother's plans, he would insist on setting a date. That was the last thing she wanted to be pressured into doing. Not until she accomplished her goal of being assigned the status of being a real reporter. She would never be satisfied until that happened.

Chapter 7

*J*udson's parents were celebrating their thirtieth wedding anniversary. They had planned a large afternoon reception, and the guest list was long and included most of the prominent people of Woodhaven. Of course, Mindy was invited. Moreover, Jamison had also assigned her to cover the event for the social page of the newspaper.

Because Mindy knew she would not have time to return home to change before the Powell's party, Mindy wore her jade-green silk dress to work. She felt self-conscious under Jamison's critical glance as she passed his desk on her way to her own. *I'm not going to explain. He should know where I'm going.* She removed her small feathered hat, put it aside, and started to go through her mail, always hoping to find another thought-provoking subject about which she could write a feature article. But nothing unusual arrived in the day's mail.

For her column, Mindy chose a letter from a young bride who complained about her mother-in-law's constant criticism. Mindy suggested that she listen politely to her husband's mother, in order to avoid conflict—and then do things her own way. Mindy could not help wondering if *she* could accept her own advice when and if she were to become Mrs. Judson Powell.

At the thought of Judson's mother, Mindy checked her pendant watch and realized she should be on her way to the party. She took her finished column to the composing room and left it on the foreman's spindle. Then, putting on her jacket and hat, she stopped by the editor's desk.

"I'm leaving now, Mr. Jamison."

He peered at her over his glasses. "This early?"

"I'm covering the Powells' anniversary," she reminded him.

He gave her a sharp glance. "Be sure you get all the names of the partygoers and spell their names right."

Even though she knew Jamison was needling her, Mindy bristled. She wasn't a rookie reporter, for heavens sake. She knew enough to cover a social event properly.

By the time Mindy reached the Powell's impressive Queen Anne house, she was still irritated with Jamison. Someday, he would have to admit she was as good and as capable as any of the male reporters.

Quite a few carriages were parked along the road in front of the house. As Mindy approached, she saw several well-dressed couples walking up the drive and mounting the steps to the front door. Judson must have been on the look-out waiting for her because as soon as she opened the gate he came running out to meet her.

"You're late. What kept you so long?" He sounded irritated. "Mother keeps asking—"

"I had to do my column and turn in my copy. I'm a working girl, don't forget."

"How could I? You never let me forget," Judson said glumly. "You know you don't have to work. It's ridiculous."

"Oh, Judson, let's not fight," Mindy begged. "Don't spoil your mother's party."

"I'm not the one who's spoiling it. She wanted us to announce our engagement today. It would be appropriate. Their anniversary; our engagement."

53

"Judson, please—"

"Oh, all right," he said, pouting. He took her arm and they went inside. He helped her off with her jacket. "Mother wants me to circulate. Will you be all right for a while?"

"Of course, I'll be just fine," Mindy assured him, looking around at the house full of people. She must be sure to get the names of the most prestigious ones, the ones who would be insulted if their names didn't appear in the society page account. "You go along."

"You're sure?" he seemed doubtful. "These are mostly my parents' friends. You won't be bored?"

"No, silly, I'll be *fine.*" No use telling Judson that she came prepared to work as well as enjoy herself. "You go on, I'll go speak to your mother."

Mrs. Powell was standing at the bottom of the ornate staircase receiving guests. She was a handsome woman, tall, with piles of silver-gold hair, a commanding carriage, beautifully groomed and gowned. Her eyes, however, were ice-blue, and Mindy often felt chilled by their penetrating gaze. Maybe it was because she felt Mrs. Powell did not approve of her. Mindy felt acutely of the disapprovel beneath her surface politeness.

Determined not to let it bother her, Mindy approached her. "Good afternoon, Mrs. Powell. What a lovely party, everything looks beautiful."

Mrs. Powell extended a hand that barely pressed Mindy's fingers. "Nice you could make it, my dear. Judson was afraid something had come up at the newspaper to delay you and you might not come. We *know* how much your *job* means to you—so much more important than a mere party."

Mindy gritted her teeth. The implied sarcasm in Mrs. Powell's tone did not escape her. She forced herself to smile sweetly. "Oh, I wouldn't have missed it," she said. She was tempted to add, "I'm covering it for the paper," but she resisted.

Mrs. Powell didn't like her. She didn't like Mindy's job, and she didn't like Mindy as her precious son's choice. She sent that as clearly as a teletype message. Well, there was nothing she could do about it. Next was Mr. Powell, who was standing beside his wife in the receiving line. He pumped Mindy's hand, greeting her with a heartiness that she guessed might be enhanced by frequent visits to the punchbowl.

After doing her duty, Mindy went into the large parlor to mingle. Two maids, uniformed in black with frilly white caps and aprons, moved through the rooms, carrying trays of canapés. For about fifteen minutes, Mindy walked around the clusters of people, recognizing most of them and surreptitiously jotting down names in the little notebook that she carried in her small beaded purse. She had become quite skilled at this sort of reporting, and she kept her pencil and pad handy. As she moved among the guests, she overheard bits and pieces of conversation. Most was banal, consisting mainly of complimentary remarks on the flowers and food. Perhaps it was her daily reading of real problems, trials, tribulations of the people who wrote to Dixie Dillon that made this banter seem so trivial. Contrary to the assurance she had given Judson, Mindy was soon bored.

What would the years ahead be like if she were to marry Judson? How many dreadful social events like this one would she have to attend? It made her shudder. Suddenly smothered under the weight of that prospect, she resisted the wild urge to leave at once. Not only would it be rude and make Judson furious, but she was also a newspaper reporter who had a job to do. As Jamison had reminded her, get all the guests' names and make sure they're spelled right.

Mindy glanced into the dining room. She hadn't taken time for lunch, so at least she could get something to eat. The food was plentiful and looked delicious. A lace cloth covered the long table, in the center of which was a silver epergne holding an elaborate centerpiece of flowers, surrounded by platters of sliced turkey and ham, jellied salads, a chafing dish of creamed shrimp, and a variety of fruits. On the sideboard were two cut glass punch bowls and matching cups, and, at either end, a coffee server, a silver teapot, and delicate china teacups.

Mindy helped herself generously to salmon mousse, several triangular sandwiches of cream cheese and watercress, and a glass of punch. She looked around for a quiet place to sit while she satisfied her hunger and mentally wrote a glowing description of this affair for the paper. She would try to write one that Mrs. Powell would be pleased to see published.

There was a bay windowed alcove adjoining the room where the Powells ate most of their meals when there was no company. Several times, especially this winter while her mother had been gone, Mindy had been invited to eat Sunday night supper with them—*en famille*, as Mrs. Powell was fond of saying. She enjoyed sprinkling French *bon mots* into ordinary conversation to impress people that she had been to Europe. Even though it had been twenty years ago, she never allowed anyone in Woodhaven to forget it.

Mindy, plate in hand, settled herself in the window seat, half-hidden by the drapery. It was there, just beside the swinging door into the pantry and kitchen, that she was handed her next big story.

Most of the guests were gathered in the parlor across the wide center hall. Mindy was relishing her food when she heard a crash, the splintering sound of breaking glass coming from the pantry. A horrified gasp was followed by an angry voice; "You idiot. Look what you've done. My best crystal," Mindy, startled, recognized Judson's mother's voice. "You stupid Irish bogtrotter. Can't you do anything right? I have a mind to fire you on the spot. Don't think you'll get a reference either. Were you raised in a pigsty? Get this swept up at once, you clumsy girl."

Mindy couldn't believe the viciousness of the tirade that continued. "And you there, Colleen. Don't stand there gawking. Get this cleaned up, and get the other glasses out and don't you dare drop a thing, you hear me?"

Mindy heard the sound of sobbing. She shrank back against the wall as the door swung open and Mrs. Powell swept out. Without seeing Mindy, she went into the hallway where more guests were arriving. Mrs. Powell quickly switch her tone, "Why, good afternoon, Mayor Bell and Loretta, dear. How nice to see you. Do come in."

Mindy reacted with first outrage at the way Mrs. Powell had talked to her servants, then contempt for her hypocrisy.–Mrs. Powell's manners were a very thin layer indeed, the refined façade ripped away by the slurs she had used toward servants. She treats her friends one way, but has an entirely different manner toward those who had no defense. Mindy's fiery indignation turned to a cold fury. She put down her plate and pushed through the swinging door into the pantry where a uniformed maid leaned against the wall, her head on her bent arm, crying. Another maid, looking frightened, was getting out more glasses with a shaky hand and carefully placing them, one by one, on a tray. When she saw Mindy, her mouth dropped open. She flushed red, "Oh, miss." She darted a glance at the sobbing girl as if to warn her.

"It's all right," Mindy said quickly. "I heard that whole thing." She took out her handkerchief and handed it to the weeping girl. "Don't worry, I'm a friend of Mr. Judson's. His mother's just upset. Big important party. I'm sure she didn't mean what she said."

The maid's face reddened more. "Oh, yes, she did, miss. She hates us Irish. We come cheap . . . that's the only reason she hires us." Her tone was bitter. "We have to stay, take her abuse—we ain't got nowheres else to go."

The skinny one who had been scolded so viciously turned timidly to look at Mindy. Her eyes widened. Tears had swollen them and her face was blotched.

"You're both new here, aren't you? Where's Emma?" Mindy asked. Emma was the Powell's housekeeper who Mindy had known for years.

"Yes, miss, we've only just come. Emma's been trainin' us, but we mostly work in the kitchen and do the cleanin' and laundry. Today was special, it was. So many people and all—"

Mindy decided to take a chance and break the secrecy about her identity. She took a deep breath and blurted out.

"Look, I'm Dixie Dillon from the newspaper. If you two tell me the truth about what it's like to be employed here, I'll write it up in the newspaper—and things will change, I promise you."

She knew she was taking a huge risk, but this could be the story she had been hoping to find. This one could surpass "What's a Girl to Do?"

Forty minutes later she hurried down the dark rear stairs, back to the warmth, the glowing lights, the sound of voices and laughter, and the clink of glasses. She pushed through the swinging door and into the Powell's bright, candlelit dining room. She blinked. She had hardly time to regain her composure when Judson appeared in the archway from the hall.

"Where've you been? I've been looking all over for you? What's the matter?"

Mindy gathered herself together and leaped upon what he'd suggested. "I'm not feeling very well, Judson. I think I might be coming down with something. I better leave."

Judson was all concern. "You do look pale. I'll take you. Sit down, wait here for a moment, until I tell Mother."

Mindy sat down on a chair actually feeling shaky. Tears stung the back of her eyes, her throat felt sore with distress. She had seen a part of life she couldn't have imagined. But she had her story.

Chapter 8

*W*hen Judson brought her back to Aunt Jen's house, Mindy, impatient to get started on her story, tried to bid him a quick goodnight, but Judson wanted to linger. At the door, he drew her into his arms.

"I missed you tonight. Where'd you wander off to anyway? I kept looking for you but kept getting trapped into conversation with Mother's friends when all I wanted was to be with you. You know what a lot of people kept asking me? When you and I were going to tie the knot? So when *are* we, Mindy?"

"Oh, Judson, it's too late to discuss this tonight. Judson, I told you, I'm really tired. It's been a long day."

He held her a moment longer, then reluctantly released her, "Oh, well, all right. But *I* want to know too. I'm tired of saying goodnight. I want us to be married, Mindy. Why can't we set a date?"

Judson sighed then bent down ready to kiss her. Instinctively, Mindy pulled away not sure exactly why. "Better not, Judson, I think I may be getting a cold and—"

"You've always got some excuse." Judson sounded offended. "Sometimes, I wonder if—"

She put her fingers on his lips cutting off his protest. "Judson, please. A lot has happened to me this year, I'm just not ready to make any decisions now."

He started to say something else then changed his mind. "All right." Reluctantly he released her. "But, Mindy, soon we're going to have talk about it. I love you. I don't want to wait much longer."

Mindy was contrite. "I know, Judson. Tonight's just not a good time to discuss things." She reached up and gave him a peck on the cheek. "I'm just too tired. It's been a long day." She knew he had been looking forward to having some time alone with her after the party and was disappointed.

He would have been even more disappointed if he had seen what happened once Mindy shut the door. Her usual energy returned. She hurried into the room she shared with Aunt Jen's sewing machine, fabric and remnants of material. She flung off her jacket, hat and gloves, then lit the lamp on the small table that served as her desk wedged between her aunt's dress form and the window and went to work. Sitting down with pen in hand, she began to retrace the entire episode at the Powell's party.

The maid who had been scolded was named Caitlin, the other one had told her. They had come over from Ireland by steerage three years before. They had been in an orphanage until they reached the age of fifteen when they were turned out to fend for themselves. An employment agency had placed them as domestics.

"Where do you sleep?" Mindy asked .

The two girls looked at each other then Colleen asked shyly, "Want to see?"

Mindy followed the two up to the second floor, along a softly carpeted hallway. As they passed Mrs. Powell's half-open bedroom door, Mindy stopped to peek into it.

It was all rose and cream, with ruffled curtains, a chaise lounge scattered with embroidered pillows. A mirrored dressing table reflected rows of crystal perfume bottles and a silver set of brush, comb, and hairpin box.

Down the hall, Mindy stopped again to peer into another room whose door had been left wide open. The furniture was rich mahogany, with a comfortable leather chair before a fireplace and hunting prints on the wall. It must be Judson's.

Colleen held a door open at the end of the hall. "This way miss."

Mindy looked through to a dark stairway leading up. Each worn, narrow step creaked as they went up. At the top she paused, surveying the low-ceilinged attic. The servants' quarters. What a contrast!

The room the two young girls shared held an iron bedstead with a bare ticking mattress, a small bureau, some hooks along the walls, one straight chair. A tiny crucifix probably brought with them hung over the bed,—Mindy knew the Powells were Presbyterians. Mindy glanced around, feeling heartsick. This bleak space was where they escaped to from the drudgery of their day.

Mindy began to write with passionate speed. As she wrote, tears rolled down her cheeks and fell onto the pages of lined paper. If this didn't touch the hardest of hearts she would lose faith altogether in the human capacity to sympathize with someone else's situation.

It was nearly one o'clock when she finally finished her first draft. She flexed her fingers, stiff from gripping her pen. Her neck ached, and she arched her back and stretched. She was drained from the hours of writing. But she had the feeling this was the best she'd ever written. In her mind, she dared Jamison not to print it. She still had to compose the letter, supposedly written by one of these Irish maids, to Dixie Dillon. She would do that tomorrow.

Mindy yawned. Her column was due on Wednesday, the day before publication.

She crawled into her own bed and drew the warm quilt over her. Before she closed her weary eyes she thought of Colleen and Caitlin huddled together on that narrow cot in their attic room and knew she would never take anything for granted again.

The Woodhaven Courier
Dixie Dillon

Dear Miss Dillon,
I am writin' this to you because I'm scared, and I'm thinkin' you mebbe could help. Me and my friend are in service in one of the big houses in this town. I try to do me best and do what the missus wants done, but she yells at us so that it makes me nervous, and then I'm clumsy and break things. That do make it worse. She gets real angry. She says if *I* don't do better, I'll have to leave with no reference. I think I done better since I first came, but if she throws me out with no reference, where can I go? Who will hire me? I don't have no family, just an old Granny back home in Ireland. I was put in an orphanage by my Pa after me Ma died. But the sisters don't keep us girls after we're fifteen. I don't know what to do. Can you help me?
Signed,
Colleen O'Casey

Mindy nearly wept over the letter she had composed. While she had written it she had felt every word. How could it not soften the stoniest heart? Dixie's answer followed.

A Long Way from Home

Imagine yourself awakened by the sound of the wind whistling through a broken window pane partially covered with a piece of cardboard. It is still dark outside. It is 4:30 in the morning—time for the maid, a fifteen-year-old immigrant girl from Ireland, to get up. The residents of the comfortable, three-story house, in the best residential section of our town, are still asleep in their beds under eiderdown quilts. When they finally do awaken, their bedrooms will be cozy with cheery fires in the grate laid and started. The girl gets out of her narrow iron bed with its hard mattress, shivering. She puts her bare feet on the cold carpetless floor. Her day has begun.

That day is a round of endless tasks. First one is to stoke the kitchen stove so breakfast can be cooked. Then water needs to be pumped and heated on the stove, and then heavy pails of it must be carried up two flights of stairs to each bedroom. Kitchen chores, under the direction of a sometimes irritable cook, follow. If it is a laundry day, all the beds must be stripped of linen; towels must be collected, as well as napkins, and tablecloths must be washed. These are then loaded into vats to be boiled, then washed, and hung up to dry.

When, at last, the time is nine o'clock at night, after dinner dishes are done, pots and pans scrubbed, and the kitchen put to rights, this young overworked girl drags herself up the three flights of stairs to her small unheated attic room. She is almost too tired to undress and get into bed. Wearily she pulls the tattered quilt about her shuddering shoulders. A tear or two rolls out from under her closed eyes as she whispers a prayer and thinks longingly of her old granny in that faraway Irish cottage where she once knew caring and affection so long ago.

Have the well-to-do women who hire these young girls to slave for them in their prosperous homes no shame? No compassion? Do they ever even think of the drafty rooms at the top of the house, where the wind howls through broken glass, where a single blanket and thin quilt are considered adequate covers throughout our wintry nights?

Is it not time for us, who have been blessed in so many ways, to share our providence with those less fortunate, who come to our country seeking a better life?

Friday, the day after the column came out, Mindy went to work not quite sure what to expect. She thought she detected some new respect in the eyes of the male reporters. There seemed to be an unspoken but apparent admiration in their glances. Still, it was the editor's approval she most hoped for and it came with the simple laconic statement.

"Well, you've done it this time, McClaren. Betcha we'll have all the benevolent societies in the city dancin' an Irish jig over this one."

Mindy went to her desk with a confident step. Surely she had proved herself. Certainly Jamison would assign her to another story. She started opening her morning's mail and worked diligently for the rest of the morning.

It wasn't until she had left for the day and was on her way home to Aunt Jen's that Judson's small buggy pulled to a stop alongside her. He looked white-faced and very, very angry. Before Mindy could say a word, he said tightly, "Please get in, Mindy, I want to talk to you."

Surprised, she climbed in. Staring straight ahead, Judson gave his horse a flick with his whip and they started off.

"What is it, Judson? Has something happened? Is something wrong?"

Judson finally swerved into the town park and brought the horse and buggy to a halt, then turned to her furiously.

"Would you like to explain this?" He brought the newspaper from out of his coat pocket, slamming it on the leather seat between them.

"I didn't think it needed to be explained," Mindy declared. "If you've read it, you know what I was trying to say."

"Don't you ever think of anything or anyone but yourself?"

"What do you mean? That whole article shows that I *do* think of others—those pitiful little Irish girls, for example."

"You *used* them for your own benefit. They're poor, ignorant girls. Hardly literate. They would never have said all this. You've exploited them for your own motives."

64

"If any one has exploited them its employers like your—" Mindy stopped abruptly before finishing the sentence. But the unspoken words hung there.

"Yes, Mindy. I'm, sure there's enough blame to go around. But you've also abused my mother's hospitality. While you were a guest in her house you went behind her back, sneaked upstairs, got those poor dumb girls to spill out a lot of nonsense that you then took and twisted to make it sound like—"

"Slavery? Well, that's practically what it is. Whether you think it's exaggerated or not—which it isn't—if my story gives just one employer pause about how they treat their servants or if it improves the condition of one or two of these girls, that will be worth whatever I did to get the story." She paused breathless. "I'm a reporter, Judson, whether you like it or not. I saw an injustice, a story worth telling. So I told it. That's what I do."

"Then, you don't think you owe my mother an apology?"

"An apology?" Mindy was taken aback. For the first time she realized her relationship with Judson and his family was in trouble.

"Yes, an apology. My mother isn't an unkind person. But you've made her sound like a monster," Judson said. "There's another side to every story. Have you thought of that? Or maybe you didn't want to tell it. Don't you realize women who hire these uneducated immigrants at least provide them work and a place to live? Otherwise most of them would end up on the street or worse."

"And that's something to be proud of?" Mindy's tone was scathing. "I was simply putting myself in those girls' shoes and showing it for what it is. Their lives are like prisons. No, Judson, I don't think I owe your mother or any woman who employs these girls an apology. I think they ought to mend their ways and improve their maids' living and working conditions."

"Does that justify you spying on my parents household? Did you bribe those girls? Promise them they'd become celebrities with your sensational yellow journalism." Judson's tone was bitter.

Insulted at the comparison he was making, Mindy said coldly, "Whether you like it or not, whether you accept it or not, I'm a reporter, Judson.. A reporter follows a story that's worth telling."

Judson's mouth settled into a grim line. Several conflicting emotions crossed his face. He wasn't a heartless young man. He rapped the newspaper a couple more times then said rather lamely, "Well, maybe it's all a tempest in a teapot. By next week, it'll blow over and it'll all be forgotten."

"Forgotten?" Mindy flared, "I don't want it to be forgotten. I published it so people would know just what it's like to be young, alone in the world, without resources, forced to earn a living under difficult circumstances. I want people to remember, to know me for writing this. My editor was pleased. Why aren't you?"

Caught between his mother's humiliation and the ideals of the woman he loved, Judson hesitated, trying to think of something to say.

"I'm disappointed in you, Judson. I thought you'd be proud of me. I guess I was wrong."

Judson flushed. "Well, of course, I am, in a way. It's just that—"

"Never mind. I can see you really aren't. You wish I'd never written anything. You don't care that I'm at last getting some recognition for my hard work."

"That's just it, Mindy. You don't have to work or prove anything to me. I'll support you and your whole family if it came to that. You can give up that job, the writing. I just want us to be married."

"Married? I think not, Judson. Sad but true, my story has made something crystal clear. You don't respect me or my work." Hot tears blurred Mindy's eyes.

"I love you, Mindy. I'm sorry if—"

She wiped her eyes with her fingers, shook her head, "No, Judson, if you truly loved me, you'd want me to be happy, to do the work I'm capable of, but you don't. You want me to sit in a pretty house somewhere, sip tea from a china cup, and give parties. Well, that's not for me. It never will be. Maybe I was wrong to ever let you think it could work out for us. . . . I see now, it can't."

"Don't say that, Mindy. I do want you to be happy, I want us to be happy—"

"How could we ever be happy together? We don't want the same things of our life."

Judson tossed the newspaper down and reached into his vest pocket. "Here, I've been carrying this around for weeks." He brought out a small, purple velvet jeweler's box and held it out. "Please, Mindy, accept it. More than anything in the world, I want us to be engaged." He pressed the spring and the lid flew open. A ruby solitaire flanked by two diamonds sparkled from a gray plush cushion.

Mindy blinked. Then shook her head sadly.

"No, Judson. I can't accept it. I can't marry you. We'd just make each other unhappy."

"You can't mean that, Mindy. We love each other. Right from the first I knew you were the girl for me, no matter what."

Mindy shook her head. "No, Judson. Now, please take me home."

Judson tried to argue Mindy out of her conviction. But she maintained stubbornly that it was over. They would never be engaged or married.

Crestfallen, defeated Judson finally turned the horse around and silently they drove back to her aunt's house.

"Don't get out, Judson. Don't see me to the door."

Mindy got down from the buggy and, without looking back, went into the house. When she closed the door she felt a deep sadness.

Her mother was remarrying, Farell was recovering and content in North Carolina, her expected engagement to Judson Powell was broken, what would she do now? Ironically, the headline she had chosen for her first explosive column "What's a Girl To Do?" came into her mind. Now, she was the one facing that very same question.

As it turned out, the Powells were not alone in their resentment over her most recent article. Every woman in town who had ever employed a hired girl or an Irish immigrant servant felt Dixie Dillon had overstepped the bounds of good taste. Whereas letters about the factory girls had been mostly positive, the Chronicle was suddenly besieged with negative letters. Most of them stated the same argument Judson had used in defense of his mother, that unless these unfortunate girls worked as domestics, some of them would end up on the streets.

Jamison, who valued community goodwill and opinion, gruffly told Mindy to "soft-pedal the sob-sister stuff" for a while. "Just until people calm down a little."

Indignant, Mindy wondered if she had been hoisted on her own petard. The very boldness of her column had landed her not on the front pages of the newspaper with her own by-line on important news stories but perhaps relegated forever giving advice to the lovelorn.

Chapter 9

A week went by, then two. Mindy was besieged by bouquets of flowers, with notes attached, from Judson. But nothing changed her mind. She was more and more convinced she had done the right thing. Whatever her future was to be, Judson Powell and the life he offered were not to be part of it! It wasn't his fault. She was who she was. She had just realized they were oil and water. No matter how they might try, it wouldn't mix.

It was a scary decision for her. Judson had always been there, waiting in the wings, so to speak, while she struggled to get a foothold in the profession she coveted. Now it became clear that it was a career that did not readily accommodate marriage—at least for a woman. Unfair but true.

Giving up the dream of writing was impossible. Mindy felt her ability was a God-given gift, just as much as being a musician or an artist or a chef. Even Scriptures upheld that "a man's gift makes a place for him."

She knew it was up to her to develop her gift and to use it to bring about something good. Judson didn't understand that, nor could she explain it to him. She felt the urgency, the compulsion to write her reactions to what she observed. Her empathy, sensitivity, and intuition were instinctive. Although she didn't know how, they were just there, available to her when she wrote.

In spite of the success of her column, Jamison had not given her status or pay of a full-time reporter. Even after her last column, Mindy sensed he never would. Perhaps he had some kind of bias against her as a woman that he wouldn't admit even to himself. But it was there, blocking her way.

Mindy knew she had come to a crossroads. She had to choose a direction. After her father's death, her life had changed enormously; then came Farell's health crisis, his departure with their mother, and her mother's marriage. All these unforeseen events were crucial in shaping Mindy's decision.

Since her mother had now remarried and would not be returning, the family home was sold. Farell planned to stay in North Carolina in the pleasant and healthful environment he had found there. Her other two brothers had their own lives.

Ironically, Mindy had become what she had once described in her Dixie Dillon column, "a young girl alone in the world, without resources or a home, forced to make her own living."

Late one Saturday afternoon, shortly after her break-up with Judson, feeling restless and at loose ends, Mindy went down to the newspaper office. As she entered the quiet, empty newsroom she stopped to get a cup of water from the cooler beside the door. Sipping it from a paper cup, she glanced casually at the bulletin board. There, posted along with several other notices, she saw one that seemed destined for her eyes.

WANTED: ALL-AROUND JOURNALIST AT THRIVING WEEKLY NEWSPAPER IN BEAUTIFUL SCENIC SURROUNDINGS, HEALTHFUL

ENVIRONMENT, UNLIMITED OPPORTUNITY FOR AMBITIOUS YOUNG PERSON WITH SOME REPORTORIAL EXPERIENCE. REPLY IN OWN HANDWRITING TO BYRON KARR, EDITOR, *ROARING RIVER GAZETTE*, COARSE GOLD, COLORADO.

Colorado! Out west. Like many easterners, Mindy had read glorious accounts of the western part of the country. It held a mysterious glamour of majestic beauty, adventure, and fortune for those daring enough to take a chance on the unknown. It was called "manifest destiny," and it beckoned the young and eager and fearless.

A thrill went all through Mindy. Here was the perfect answer for her damaged ego, her loneliness, her depression. A possible opening in the stone wall of her desired profession. Why not answer the ad? It had not specified *man*. It had used the word *person,* no designation of gender nor indication of discrimination against the female sex.

Mindy hurried over to her desk and immediately drafted a letter to the editor of the *Roaring River Gazette.* In her best professional style, she stated her employment of nearly a year at the *Courier,* and a summary of the stories she had covered. As she closed, she hesitated. Just in case this editor had the least bit of resistance against hiring a woman reporter, she signed her letter: *I. Howard McClaren.* It was, in truth, her name: she had been christened Independence Howard McClaren. She blotted the flourishing signature and smiled. Monday she would take it to the post office, attach the appropriate postage, and mail it to Coarse Gold, Colorado. Even the name promised excitement and adventure.

To her surprise, after returning to Aunt Jen's the next afternoon, she found a dejected Judson sitting on the porch steps. He was holding a bouquet of limp yellow daffodils, wilting fast for lack of water. At the sight of her, his face brightened. He stood up, letting the flowers drop.

"Mindy, I'm sorry. Sorry for what happened, sorry for all the things I said. Can't we forget what happened? Start over? I can't face losing you. I love you. Please, Mindy."

He looked so sad, so abject. And perhaps she was even beginning to feel a little uncertain about what she had just done. For a minute she was tempted to give in. Then something clicked inside: a warning. The longing of the moment blinds to the possibilities of regret. When she had broken her engagement, she had felt sad, but she knew it was the right thing to do. If she relented even a little now, it would have to be done all over again. And next time, it might be even more painful for both of them.

As gently as she could Mindy said, "I'm sorry, Judson, it would never work for us. I think down deep you know that too. Let's say good-bye now and still be friends. Isn't that possible?"

Judson's face clouded. "You are so stubborn, Mindy. You only see what you want to see. You're willing to give up everything we could have together for some foolish dream—"

"That's just it, Judson, foolish or not, it's *my* dream. One you don't share. And I won't give it up. I can't." She shook her head sadly. "That's why it wouldn't work." She saw the muscle in his cheek tighten, knew that he was trying to think of other ways to persuade her.

"I'm going away, Judson, leaving Woodhaven. For what it's worth, I may not find what I'm looking for, but I have to try."

Judson looked startled. "Where are you going? When?"

"I don't think I should tell you, Judson. It wouldn't matter."

His shoulders slumped. "Mindy, if only you'd—" He stopped, unable to go on, as if he couldn't even find words to say.

Mindy watched Judson go down the walk, out through the gate. It was so final. Even though her heart was breaking, she knew she had made the right choice. For both their sakes.

This last conversation closed the door forever on what might have been for them.

The letter was already on its way, though she knew it might be weeks before she heard back from the editor, Byron Karr. If she waited for his reply, she might change her mind or lose her nerve. Or worse still, perhaps the editor of the *Roaring River Gazette* would refuse to hire a woman reporter once he finds out. So, what if she just showed up?

Her heart thundering, Mindy walked to the train station and bought a one-way ticket to Coarse Gold, Colorado.

PART 2

Chapter 10

*C*oarse Gold was a misnomer. It was silver, veins of it, discovered in the surrounding mountains, that had transformed this desolate stretch of land into a town. First, it had been a rough mining camp, populated by greedy men eager to strike it rich. Soon, a meager stream of people trickled in, providing the necessities for the miners. Within a few years it had grown into a small, thriving town on the edge of civilization—with 4,000 citizens. Houses, stores, two hotels, five saloons, a newspaper and three churches followed.

With a grinding screech of metal wheels on iron tracks, the train jolted to a stop. Minutes later, Mindy stepped down from the train. Travel-worn, her mouth dry, her eyes gritty from flying cinders and soot, her hair in need of brushing, and her clothes wrinkled from the long trip— she took a quick look around. Aware of the curious stares of a group of disheveled-looking men standing across from the wooden platform, she straightened her hat brim, picked up her valise, and headed for a ramshackle building with a crooked sign on its jutting roof: THE PALACE HOTEL.

Hardly representative of its name, it seemed the most likely place to find a room, or perhaps even to take a bath or at least freshen up before going to the newspaper office.

That was her priority. Once she had secured the job, she would send someone for her trunk and find a proper room to rent. Trying to look more confident than she felt, Mindy crossed the unpaved street. Still the object of inquisitive eyes, she mounted the uneven wooden steps. At the top, as she reached for the door handle, it was opened for her. Startled, she took a step back. A man in a tweed jacket, bowed slightly, breasted his hat, then gestured toward the entrance. He was of medium height, slimly built with a lean face and thick, smooth hair. His eyes were light gray and thoughtful.

Surprised at this courtesy, the kind she had not encountered often on her long, arduous journey and certainly had not expected in this rugged frontier town, Mindy murmured her thanks and proceeded him into the hotel.

The lobby was not any more palace-like than the exterior. *Any port in a storm,* Mindy thought as she glanced quickly around her. At the registry counter a balding clerk regarded her with curiosity. "I'd like a room, please."

"One night or two?"

She hesitated. If the reporter's job were already filled? What then? There would not be another train east until the next day. She had already wisely checked with the conductor. "Two."

He took a rusty key from the board behind him and handed it to her. A tattered cardboard tag attached to it bore the number *"7."* "Up them steps, first room on the left," he pointed to a wide, rather crooked staircase.

"Could you please tell me where the *Roaring River Gazette* is located?"

Before the clerk answered, a voice behind her spoke. "It's just down the street at the corner, to your left as you come out the hotel."

Mindy turned to see it belonged to the same gentleman who had opened the hotel door for her.

"Thank you," she said, wondering who he was. He certainly did not look, dress, or behave like the other residents she had observed on her way from the train station. Did he even lived in Coarse Gold? But then, how else could he have known where the newspaper office was? Of course, it wouldn't do to ask.

As if reading her mind, he replied, "I've just come from the *Gazette*. My uncle is the editor."

What a coincidence! Mindy would have dearly loved to find out more about the man she was about to ask for a job, query his nephew about her chances, and discover if there was any prejudice against hiring a woman. But again, she didn't dare. It would have been unseemly. It might give this stranger the right to take liberties that would have been improper. Although he had the manners of a gentleman, a woman alone could not be too careful of giving the wrong impression. So Mindy merely nodded, took her key, picked up her valise, and climbed the uneven stairs to her room.

She shouldn't have expected much from the room, considering the general condition of the hotel. Still, she felt dismayed as she entered and glanced around. It contained a bed, a washstand, and a rickety chair. This was as bad as the attic room inhabited by the Irish maids she had described in her Dixie Dillon column. Dust was everywhere, a fine powdery beige on everything. Mindy did not dare try out the bed. She would face that later. First, she must present herself to Byron Karr, the editor of the *Roaring River Gazette*.

She washed off as much of the grime from the train trip as possible in the lukewarm water, poured from a pitcher into the small bowl. All Mindy could think was, *What would mother's aunties say to this?* Since, their standard was "Cleanliness is next to godliness," they would be scandalized for sure. Before she left Woodhaven, she had been the recipient of all sorts of cautionary advice, dire warnings, and heartfelt pleas to change her mind—all from a wide contingent of her mother's relatives. All fell on deaf ears. Mindy was determined not to turn back. Whatever her own reservations about her rash decision—made in the grip of disappointment, disillusionment, and loneliness— she honestly felt her destiny lay elsewhere. Somewhere far from Woodhaven her dream awaited.

She had sold many of the treasured belongings left in the McClaren house to pad out her traveling expenses, insuring that she would have enough money in case she met with any emergencies—or, heaven forbid, when she arrived in Colorado and did not get the job. It was a possibility she wouldn't consider and one she certainly did not share with her worried relatives.

The day she left, Mindy's chest had felt like a heavy stone. Her sadness at leaving these loving people, who had known her since she was born, had been too deep for tears. For their sakes, she had tried to act sure of herself and composed, afraid that she might show her own fear that, as many of them said, she was making a mistake. At the station she had gone from one to the other, hugged and kissed them, and was showered with farewell gifts. Baskets of fruit, fried chicken, and hard-boiled eggs had been thrust upon her as though she would starve on the trip otherwise.

Mindy had pressed her face against the train window to keep the picture of the little group, waving damp handkerchiefs at the end of the station platform, in her view as long as possible.

Actually, the food had come in handy. On the harrowing trip across the prairie, the train made only short stops, during which the passengers could stretch their legs and rush to get something to eat. Makeshift restaurants—actually weather-beaten shacks—provided tough, greasy meat, hard bread, and warm beer to the desperate travelers. As a result,

Mindy was sure she had lost weight in the days she had been on the train.

Now she had arrived. She had survived the trip. Someday, she decided, she might even write about both the frightening moments and the hilarious incidents that she had experienced. But right now, her next step was to present herself at the newspaper office.

Outside, on the hotel porch, several roughly dressed men, miners perhaps, lounged in chairs tilted on the back legs leaned against the wall. They all jolted upright as Mindy stepped out the door. A few stood up, touching the brims of battered felt hats. Mindy inclined her head in acknowledgment of the politeness. As she stood at the top of the steps for a minute, one grizzly bearded man spoke. "The *Gazette*'s jest down the street to your right, ma'am, can't miss it."

Another one jerked his thumb left, "Jest 'crost the road from the general store and Doc Mason's office."

Mindy had all she could do not to laugh out loud. Already her purpose for being here had made the rounds, probably from the hotel clerk. The man who had identified himself as the editor's nephew, she suspected, was too much of a gentleman to have spread the news. Nodding her thanks, Mindy went down the steps, turned left, and walked down the board sidewalk.

She soon found herself in front of a grayed frame building on which was posted a slightly askew sign identifying it as THE ROARING RIVER GAZETTE.

Her heart thumped wildly as she turned the doorknob. She walked into a dimly lit, cluttered room. At one end, a man sat at a roll-top desk stacked high with papers. Mindy stood there for a full minute before he seemed to be aware that someone had entered. He half-turned, his spindle-back chair squeaking noisily as it swiveled.

"Mr. Karr?" she said, trying not to sound tentative.

"The same," he replied in a husky voice.

She picked her way through the obstacle course of the room to his desk. As she got close, she could see he had tousled brownish hair and at least a two-day stubble of a beard on his deeply lined face. He was without a jacket, wearing suspenders over a rumpled shirt with the sleeves rolled up. He looked at Mindy with bloodshot eyes and in a slightly slurred voice asked, "Well, what can I do for you, young lady?"

Mindy's heart sank. Had he been drinking?

"I've come about the reporter's job."

His bushy eyebrows rose alarmingly. He straightened up from his slumped position and gave her a long, evaluating look. "The position's already been filled. In fact, I was just sending out the acceptance letter to someone called—" He glanced down at the paper on his desk, adjusted his glasses, which had slipped down on his nose, and read, "Howard McClaren."

Relief swept over Mindy. "That is I. I'm Howard McClaren," she said. Then smiled, "That's *me.* No, I mean *I.*"

The editor stared at her. "You?"

His glance moved over her small, slender build, her shining blue, long-lashed eyes, her eager smile.

"Yes, sir, I am Howard McClaren. I wrote to you nearly a month ago and not having heard back, I assumed that the best thing to do was to come in person."

The editor shuffled through a pile of papers in his wire basket and brought out the letter Mindy recognized as hers. The one in which she had stated her qualifications for a reporter's job and given her credits, including some tear sheets of her two Dixie Dillon columns. He tapped the letter with bent knuckles and demanded, "And all this background experience in newspaper work is true?"

"Yes, sir."

Karr was still holding the letter, his eyebrows drew together in a fierce frown. "What's the 'I' stand for?" he growled. Mindy raised her chin defensively. "Independence."

The editor's mouth twitched in a futile effort not to smile. He stroked his chin, "And are you? Independent?"

"I try to be. In the best sense of that word. I try to be responsible, punctual, and meet my deadlines."

"Well, I guess you are—comin' all this way on a chance that the job was still open and that I might even hire you. How'd you know I don't think a newspaper's no place for a woman?" he looked at her sharply. "I reckon you must have some gambler in you to do that." He paused, picked up her letter and studied it for a long minute. Then a grin cracked his seamed face. He squinted up at her. "Well, I guess that's good enough for me, Independence Howard McClaren. I guess you'll do. When can you start?"

Chapter 11

"Tomorrow," Mindy gasped.

"Fine. Be here at eight." Karr reached for his coat jacket on the back of his chair. "I'd show you around the place, but my nephew's leaving for San Francisco this afternoon, and I've got to see him off."

"I understand. Tomorrow will be just fine."

"Tomorrow will be time enough. Friday's pretty slow. We put the paper to bed yesterday, and Pete's gone fishin', I expect, and who knows what that rascal Timmy is up to. You'll meet 'em and get to know 'em soon enough."

Karr stood up, picked up his jacket and started toward the door. Then, as an afterthought, turned back and said, "You got a place to stay?"

"I took a room at the Palace Hotel."

Karr made a face. "That's no place for a lady. Go to Mrs. Busby's boarding house. Clean rooms, good food, safe. A lot of miners come in from the hills on weekends and go to the Palace. The place can get rowdy, and the music goes on until the wee hours. Those fellows carouse all night. It's not unusual to see a couple of brawls and people thrown out into the street." The editor shook his head. "As I said, no place for a lady." Karr shrugged into his jacket. "Come on. I'll take you over and get you settled. Got luggage?"

"Yes, I left my trunk at the station. I thought I'd leave it there until I was sure—"

"Well, you're sure now."

"Yes, thank you. I can't tell you—"

"Don't bother. You've still got to prove yourself."

"I know, I just—"

Karr pulled out his pocket watch. "Good grief, that train's due to leave in fifteen minutes. Can you wait until it goes? I'm supposed to meet my nephew there."

"Please go ahead. You don't want to miss seeing your nephew off. I have to go back to the hotel, pick up my baggage check."

"Good enough," he grinned. "Your name suits you, Miss Independence."

Mindy hurried back to the hotel, up to her room, retrieved her claim ticket, repacked her valise. The desk clerk eyed her suspiciously when she checked out.

"You still have to pay for the half-day you used the room," he grumbled.

"Of course." She handed over the money and then, with as much dignity as she could manage, walked out with her head high.

She got to the station just as the train was ready for departure. She spotted Karr and his nephew, whom she had already met at the Palace Hotel, standing on the platform. Karr introduced them, but the shriek of the train whistle drowned out his voice so Mindy did not catch his nephew's name. He smiled pleasantly, however, and said, "Pleased to meet you, Miss McClaren."

A few minutes later, amidst the swirling steam just as the train was beginning to move, he swung up the train steps, waving his arm, and then disappeared into the car. Mindy stood there with Karr until the train rounded the bend.

"Come on, now. I'll get someone to tote your trunk, and I'll take you over to Mrs. Busby's."

Mrs. Busby turned out to be a motherly soul who gave Mindy a long, evaluating look at first, and then gladly took her under her proverbial wing. She gave Mindy a room on the second floor at the back of the house and told her briskly, "You'll want a nice quiet place to come after a day at Mr. Karr's newspaper. You can get your breakfast and supper here, but for the midday meal you're on your own." She winked at Mindy and, lowering her rather strident voice, added, "I takes my nap then. Need it. Up at four and in the kitchen cooking; then supper preparation begins at four in the afternoon."

Mindy spent the rest of the day getting settled in. It had all worked out much better than she could have imagined. Her impulsiveness in coming to Coarse Gold had paid off. Of course, she didn't know what she would have done if Byron Karr had not hired her.

Mindy did have a few bad moments, however, as she unpacked her trunk and came upon the mementos she had brought with her. They didn't amount to much, because most of the furnishings, bric-a-brac, and other family belongings had been shipped to her mother in North Carolina. The rest of the family possessions, at least those that Tom and Emily had not taken to their new home, had been sold with the old house. Still, handling the few small things she had chosen to keep brought unexpected tears.

There was the little porcelain clock from her bedroom, the brush and comb set her parents had given her for her sixteenth birthday, the book of Farell's poetry he had hand lettered and bound for her. Farell, her dearest friend and confidant, how she missed him and would go on missing him for the rest of her life. But she knew he was happy where he was and she had to go on her own path. Perhaps, some day, when she was a famous journalist . . . Mindy smiled at her own foolishness. Sighing, she put her special belongings in her new room and was immediately filled with excitement. What an adventure this would be, and she meant to savor every minute of it.

That evening when the a cow bell clanged loudly at six, Mindy went downstairs to the dining room. Mindy felt a dozen pair of eyes turn on her. There were two long tables and on each side sat a row of men. She was taken aback. Were all Mrs. Busby's boarders men? Probably. Not many single women came west alone to take a job usually occupied by a man.

Mrs. Busby, red-faced from the kitchen heat, came bustling in with a tray containing huge platters of chops and bowls piled with mashed potatoes and beans. After setting them down on the table, she announced in her loud voice, "Now take a good look, gentlemen. This young lady is a new employee of the *Gazette,* and Mr. Karr don't want her gettin' no hasslin' from nobody. She's a special lady, and we want her to be comfortable and happy. And I won't take none of your pranks nor silly doin's, you hear me?"

There was a murmur from both tables. Mrs. Busby waited, hands on hips, for her words to sink in. Mindy felt her cheeks flame under the scrutiny before everyone lowered their eyes. Then Mrs. Busby ordered, "All right now, plow in." The men immediately began passing bowls and piling their plates full.

Mrs. Busby came over to where Mindy stood at the doorway, uncertain of where she should sit. Her quandary was soon resolved when Mrs. Busby said, "Mr. Karr's coming over to eat with you tonight. He thought it might be easier for you this first time, and he had some things about the paper to discuss with you."

Gratefully, Mindy followed her to one of the smaller tables that ringed the dining room. It was set for two. She didn't have long to wait until Byron, his hair slicked down wearing a freshly laundered shirt, arrived.

Right away, Mindy discovered Byron Karr was an educated man who knew the newspaper business. How he had ever ended up here in this isolated Colorado town was a mystery. Their conversation went well. Byron sketched some of his hopes for the expansion of the paper to a biweekly as the town grew.

"Of course, that pretty much depends on how long the silver holds out. Some of the mines have been emptied. There may be others with rich veins no one has yet discovered. Even if the silver goes, this town has other possibilities, in my opinion. Pure air, good healthy climate, room for people with ambition and goals. The west still has a long way to go, but back east people are getting the idea that here is where a man can make his own way—or a woman, for that matter."

As Byron talked, Mindy felt an anticipatory thrill. She knew that this was a chance of a lifetime. To work with someone who knew the newspaper business from the inside out.

Chapter 12

From that first day at the *Gazette*, Mindy's days were filled with a variety of jobs Byron assigned to her. She met Pete, the printer, a man of indiscriminate age, round shouldered, keen eyed, with gnarled hands and ink-stained fingernails. With a stub of a pipe clenched in his mouth, his permanently wrinkled brow gave his face a quizzical expression. When Byron brought Mindy back to the composing room, Pete gave her a curt nod and a cautious look.

Next to be introduced was Timmy, the snub-nosed, four-teen-year old "printer's devil." He was learning the trade and doing everything around the newspaper office that needed doing: sweeping, emptying the trash, running errands, and the folding of the paper on publication day, a job for which Mindy was also recruited. While they worked together, she learned Timmy was an orphan. He lived in a back room of one of the saloons—a kindness shown him by the bar owner. Timmy was extraordinarily bright and perennially cheerful—which was a nice contrast because Pete was often grumpy and Byron . . . well, Byron was sometimes "not himself." At least, that was the most tactful way

Mindy could express it. By the time she had been in Coarse Gold a month, she had learned that Thursday, after the paper had been printed, Byron usually went on a serious drinking binge. Most of the time, he crossed the street and disappeared into the Golden Slipper. Occasionally, it was the Friendly Spur. Other times he simply disappeared.

Timmy explained all this to her. She had met Timmy one day coming out of one of the saloons, carrying a bottle to take back to Byron at the office. Her face must have shown her shock at a man sending a boy on such an errand because the youngster quickly defended the editor. "Mr. Karr is a trump. Most of the time, anyways. And when he's drinkin', the boss don't get mean or ugly like some do. He don't get into fights, nothin' like that. Don't harm no one, just gets quietly drunk."

Mindy was learning a new kind of tolerance. In Woodhaven, such a man would be ostracized, his behavior condemned. Whatever hidden demons Byron had, the oblivion afforded by alcohol seemed to fend them off. As Timmy had pointed out, he didn't hurt anyone—but himself. On Mondays, even if a little heavy-lidded and haggard, Byron was always at his desk, sorting through his copy and ready to prepare the next edition.

One Tuesday morning, Byron asked Mindy. "Think you're ready for a big assignment?"

Never knowing when Byron was teasing, "Of course," Mindy answered, hoping, maybe it would be something like a court case. But his next words dashed that hope.

"Community meeting tonight. Eight o'clock. Town hall."

Anyway, it was her first assignment in the official role as a reporter for the *Gazette*. The article would actually be printed in the paper. She would have to take accurate notes, be factual, no flights of fantasy as in her old Dixie Dillon column. The town's people who attended would each have their own axe to grind, a point of view they wanted to project. They would all be listening to the speeches and getting their own impressions of what was taking place. If any of the proceedings they had witnessed were not correct, the reporter would be blamed and the paper vilified. Byron assured her that Coarse Gold people had no problem speaking their minds.

Until now Mindy had not gone out as a reporter. She had spent most of her time in the newspaper building learning the ropes. Other than the few advertisers to whom Byron had sent her to check ad copy and collect fees, Mindy had not met many people from the community.

At seven-thirty she entered the big, drafty building. Little knots of people, gathered in groups, were catching up on gossip and discussing recent events, which would be debated and voted on that night.

Mindy smiled timidly at one or two folks who caught her glance. Then she looked around for a seat, one near the front so that she could hear everything that was going on and take notes verbatim. A long table and five chairs were placed in front for the councilmen. At eight sharp a big, barrel-chested man with a sandy bush of a beard, strode up to the front, took his place behind the table, and lifted a gavel. He brought it down hard. "This meeting will now come to order." The murmur of voices quieted. People found seats, late-comers wandered in, and sat down in back as the meeting got under way.

Mindy took notes as fast as she could, while she worried that she might miss something important. It was impossible to record everything everyone said on both sides of an issue. Each speech was interrupted and objected to, and the loudest voice often prevailed in the arguments that followed. By the time the evening was over, she had a pounding headache and a quivering knot in her stomach. How could she ever write this up? She remembered one thing she had learned at her old job in Woodhaven: "Get all the names of anyone who spoke and spell them right." At least she could do that.

She approached the chairman and introduced herself. "Well, howdy, miss. I heard Karr had hired a gal—I mean a lady—at the *Gazette*." His gaze swept over her, taking in the small, feathered hat and the stylish jacket, and thinking, *Karr sure knows how to pick 'em.*

With his admiring glance, Mindy realized her appearance might work against her. She would never be taken seriously unless she was very professional. She drew herself up to her full height and asked for a list of names of the people who had spoken on the agenda.

At first, the chairman seemed flustered by her business-like manner, but he handed over a paper on which the speakers had written their own names. After that he seemed to regain his joviality. He pumped her hand, thanked her for coming. "Nice to have met you, ma'am."

On her way back to the office, Mindy felt a prickle of pride. She had accomplished her task and also made the impression that she was a real working reporter.

The town meeting was duly written up and appeared in the next edition of the *Gazette*. Since nobody complained and no irate letters to the editor came in the mail, Mindy felt she had passed the first hurdle in her life as a reporter in Coarse Gold.

By the end of two month Mindy felt she had been in Coarse Gold for ages—as if no other life had existed before she went to work at the *Gazette*.

One Friday, Mindy was working alone in the newspaper office. Byron had vanished right after press time the day before. She knew now he would be unreachable for the weekend. She liked having the place to herself. It was usually such a beehive of noise and activity. This gave her time to catch up on some of the material that came across her desk. She was trying to come up with a feature. She thought Byron might like her to do something distinctive, something that would be her unique contribution to the paper. Not like Dixie Dillon, but maybe "One Woman's Opinion"—a mixture of ideas and reflections. She would approach him on a good day—and very tactfully.

She suspected that, underneath, Byron still had some reservations about a woman being a reporter. She discovered that there had been no other applicants for the job when she appeared on the scene—so he had been desperate and hired her. Now, she wanted to show him she was worth taking on.

She had written a few things but wasn't sure how they would look in print. She had watched set type Pete often enough. Could she maybe do it?

She got up from her desk and went back to the print shop. On press day Mindy was fascinated by the way Pete and Timmy moved around doing all the varied tasks necessary to get the paper out. Of course, Timmy had all the dirty jobs: washing the forms and inky presses, cleaning and refilling the ink plates, keeping the rollers clean, gathering the discarded paper from the floor, and taking it out to the burn barrels behind the building.

On the other hand, Pete was a skilled craftsman. Sitting up on his high stool, his hands moved effortlessly. With the printer's stick, a short, shallow, metal tray held in his left hand, he assembled the type, letter by letter, line by line, until he had a stickful—about a dozen lines. Then he transferred that type into a long steel tray, called the galley, and started over with an empty stick. An experienced compositor, like Pete, had long ago "learned the case"—that is, where to reach for each letter, space, and punctuation mark. The type was kept in shallow wooden trays, called cases, separated into boxes for the individual letters. There were two cases, one for the small letters, the other for capitals.

The two cases were set on a rack with the small letters immediately in front and the capitals just beyond and tilted up at an angle.

Pete made it look easy. He never seemed to hurry. He would casually glance at the copy to be set, read a line then, with a click-click-click, he set the letters in the stick. All the lines seemed to fill and be spaced properly as if by magic. Pete could even carry on a conversation while he was setting type.

Mindy was in awe of another skill that Pete possessed: his ability to read type upside down, from left to right, and from the bottom up, line by line. Type, of course, is backwards—it shows the reverse of how the actual printed letters will appear.

As Mindy wandered around the composing room, looking at everything in Pete's domain, she heard the creak of the front door opening. She peeked around the corner to see who had come in. A tall figure filled the door frame, a young man with a rangy build. He had a strong-jawed face and blunt handsome features. His eyes were very blue in a deeply tanned face. At the sight of Mindy in the door of the composing room, he removed his wide-brimmed hat and shook back his thick locks of sandy hair from his broad forehead.

He wore a leather vest over his a blue denim shirt. Around the waist of his dark pants was slung a gun holster. For a minute Mindy wondered if this was a hold-up—the kind she'd read about in the more lurid penny dreadful Westerns her brothers had read when younger. Then she saw a large metal star on his leather vest. A law man!

In spite of it, Mindy felt a sharp stab of alarm. In Woodhaven, the appearance of an officer of the law meant trouble. Had Byron been drunk and disorderly contrary to Timmy's stout defense? Or had something happened to old Pete? Perhaps Tim had an accident?

"Afternoon, ma'am." He spoke with a soft Texas drawl.

"Good afternoon," Mindy replied.

"Byron around?"

"No, I'm afraid not, Can I help you?"

"Well, I dunno. Who's in charge around here?"

Mindy wiped her hands on a greasy cloth and followed his glance around the room. "I guess I am."

His eyes widened in surprise, then narrowed as his gaze came back to her. She was amused by the look of doubt and surprise.

"This is about something for the paper—" He looked down at a sheaf of paper he held.

"Let me see what you have. If it's for the next edition, I'll have to check to see if we have room for it."

He hesitated. "Don't you need Byron's okay?"

"Well, since he's not here, and not likely to be until Monday, it looks like it's up to me. Of course, if it's not all that important—" She shrugged and started to turn away.

"Oh, yes ma'am, it's important all right. Doggoned important, I mean, excuse me, miss, what I mean to say is—well, you see, I'm the marshal hereabouts. Taylor Bradford's the name. These here are Wanted posters."

With a small frown of annoyance, Mindy turned back to him. "Want me to check, then decide what we can do with them?"

Taylor took a second look at this woman with the assured attitude. She was only a little over five foot and pretty—about the prettiest young woman he had seen in a month of Sundays. She had small, neat features, eyes so bright and blue they reminded him of wild summer berries. But she did not seem to give a fig for her appearance. Her auburn hair was piled up haphazardly with a pencil stuck in its topknot. There was a smudge of ink on her cheek, and she was wearing a printer's apron. Besides that, she had a high-and-mighty air about her that was off-putting.

Taylor shifted from one foot to the other uneasily. Byron was probably off on a binge and had left this gal running the show! It hadn't happened in quite a spell, his fallin' off the wagon. But this had to be the dumbest thing he'd done, leaving the newspaper in the hands of this little slip of a girl.

"Well, I'd say these are as important as anything Byron would put in the paper." He smiled as he held out a bundle of posters. His attempt at humor fell flat. Mindy's expression remained distant.

He tried to sound more official. "I just come back from territory headquarters in Boulder. These here are pictures of some outlaws we're lookin' for. Some of the meanest fellas you ever'd want to see. I'm sure Byron'd agree that these are ..." He paused, wondering if he should say any more. This gal was being pretty high-handed as if she might not print them. Taylor cleared his throat "Byron usually puts three or four in the newspaper in case someone recognizes them—"

"I see. Well, I'll take them, and when Byron comes in he can make the decision. Where are they usually placed?"

"On the back sheet. That's so folks who can't read good or don't care to read the other stuff in the paper can see them, and—"

"I understand." Mindy cut him off to show her disdain for the opinion that *anyone* would *not* find the *Gazette* compelling reading.

Taylor shifted from one foot to the other uneasily. Then, since there seemed no reason to stay, he took a tentative step backward. "Much obliged, miss—ah, I don't believe I caught your name?"

"McClaren," Mindy supplied shortly.

"Well, then ..." Taylor twisted his hat in his hands. "Thank you, Miss McClaren." He moved awkwardly back through the newsroom and out the door. "Nice to have made your acquaintance."

But Mindy had already returned to the composing room.

On the steps, Taylor replaced his hat, thinking what an unusual encounter that had been. That Miss McClaren made a fellow feel downright uncomfortable. He'd always gotten on good with ladies. He'd been raised right by a Texan grandmother and knew how to treat women with gracious courtesy. But Miss McClaren was different. Different from the saloon girls with their bold eyes, painted smiles, and easy banter. There weren't hardly any decent single women in Coarse Gold—or any of the other towns hereabouts. It was plain she was a lady. But different. Taylor had never run into anyone like her before. She was doggoned sure of herself. Besides, unlike most of the ladies he'd encountered in these parts, she hadn't seemed impressed by the star he wore so proudly.

Taylor shook his head. Still there was something about her . . . a smile tugged at his mouth. Wonder if she rode? He might ask her to go riding some time. That might be how he'd get to know her some. He had a sweet little mare he'd just broke, perfect for a lady. When Byron got back, he'd amble by, casual like. He and Byron got along just fine. Maybe that would give him a chance to get more acquainted with Miss McClaren.

Chapter 13

D earest Mama and Farell,

I can't believe I have been in Coarse Gold nearly four months. I know I have been remiss in writing to you, but I have been so busy and am learning so much about the business of putting out a newspaper. I am so tired at the end of the day, it is all I can do to eat supper and fall into bed. Now, of course, there are some evening meetings, which Mr. Karr has me attend in order to write a report for the paper. People here depend on the news they read in the *Gazette*—so it's important.

I am quite nicely settled here at Mrs. Busby's boarding house. She is a motherly soul and takes great interest in all her boarders' lives. I have a feeling she would not hesitate to give advice or a reprimand to anyone she felt needed it. I've overheard her lecture some of the miners after a riotous weekend. The curious thing is that these big, hefty men take it like lambs. So far I have not been the recipient of one of her scoldings. But I'm prepared if that time comes.

My room is spacious and comfortable, with many reminders of home: the log cabin quilt Aunt Lu made for me on the bed, the family picture we had taken the last

Christmas Pa was alive, my favorite books and my Bible. There are three large windows so that every time I look up, I see the magnificent view.

I wish I could describe what it is all like. I will try anyway. Colorado is so different from the landscape we are used to— and certainly different from where you two are now in North Carolina, where everything is lush and green. This is desert country, but it has its own stark beauty.

Mindy stopped writing. She gazed out the window over the table in her bedroom. She could see the long sloping valley of soft, gray sage stretch to the distant purplish rim of the hills. The sky was a vast azure blue. Even in this short time, she had come to love it here. True, she had not yet known the icy winds, the intense cold, and the heavy snow of the Colorado winters that she had been warned about. Nor had she yet experienced the furnace-like heat of summer when a brassy sun bleached the grass and dried the wells. So far she had only known the mild autumn. Still she felt a deep happiness at having found her place. Almost from the first, she had the strange premonition that, here, all her dreams would come true.

After Taylor Bradford first met Mindy, he often seemed to find a great deal of sheriff's business to discuss with the editor of the *Gazette*. Although he would lower his six-foot-three lean body into the chair by Byron's desk, his gaze was usually fixed on the small auburn-haired lady at the next one. Byron didn't miss the sheriff's attraction to his new assistant, and he teased Mindy unmercifully about it.

Taylor always announced his departure in a louder than necessary voice and took his time getting to his feet. If Mindy didn't look up from her work to acknowledge him, he made a point of stopping by her desk. One day, when Taylor had failed to engage Mindy in conversation after several attempts, he took a reluctant leave, looking disappointed.

When Taylor exited, Byron leaned back in his chair and laughed long and heartily. "Why don't you give that poor fella the time of day, Mindy? Anyone can see he's longing for a kind word from you."

"Byron, you're wrong. Wrong about me, and wrong about Sheriff Bradford. He's just being polite. That's his Texas style. He's not interested in me. And I'm certainly not interested in him."

One thing Mindy didn't know about the soft-spoken Texan, however, was his tenacity. He didn't take her indifference as permanent. After all, his reputation was that he got whatever he went after.

Among the many jobs Byron passed on to Mindy was the proper wording and laying out of ads. Late Friday afternoon, the town's undertaker, Phileas Proctor, brought in the handwritten notice he had composed for his establishment. "I want it in a prominent place. So's nobody can miss it," he told Byron.

After he left, Mindy and Byron read the poorly thought-out copy and had a good laugh. "Quite an enterprising entrepreneur, wouldn't you say?" joked Byron. "I'm grateful for the advertising revenue, but such an ad has a limited clientele. He can't get testimonies from any satisfied customers, now can he?" He handed the copy to Mindy. "Here, see what you can do with this."

Mindy put it aside until after the weekly paper had been put to bed, was out, and delivered. She needed more time to think about the most tasteful way of putting all the ideas Mr. Proctor wanted incorporated.

Since Mr. Proctor wanted it to go in the next edition, Mindy went in late Saturday afternoon when everyone else was gone, the building empty and quiet, to work on it.

Mr. Proctor's list of services offered by the funeral parlor were given in a hodge-podge manner. Mindy's job was to put them in some order. Across the top of the ad, Mr. Proctor wanted a boldface heading "HAVING YOUR SAY ABOUT YOUR LAST DAY." To Mindy, this seemed too blunt. Still, since he was paying for the ad and the best position in the paper, she would try her best.

She carefully read what Mr. Proctor had written on his list: the casket prices from "fine imported mahogany you'd be proud of" down to the cheapest one of plain, unvarnished pine "you wouldn't want to be seen dead in." Mindy shook her head and laughed. If she didn't know better, she could think Mr. Proctor was joking. "Selected fabrics for lining if you so desire. Your choice of religious services. We can make arrangements if you are not able to do so. We have printed eulogies to choose from, or poetry to be read at the gravesite. You can write your own obituary beforehand to be sent to relatives back east—highly recommended."

Mindy remembered Byron's quip at that final sentence phrase: "Highly recommended?" he had hooted. "By whom?"

With a sigh Mindy took a fresh piece of paper and began putting the ad together. Neatly, she printed out the items in their logical order. She was making the final arrangement of the layout when she realized it was getting dark. She lit the oil lamp and brought it to her desk. She wasn't sure just how long she had been working when there was a knock on the newspaper door. Who could it be? Maybe Byron had seen the light and come to investigate? She got up and carrying the lamp went to the door. Through the windowed upper half she saw the outline of a tall male figure. A familiar Texas drawl identified him, "Taylor Bradford, Miss McClaren."

Mindy unlocked the door, and opened it. "Is anything wrong?" "No, ma'am, not a thing. I was just concerned some when I saw the light burning in here. Knowin' nobody works on the paper from Thursday until Monday."

"I had a special job I needed to do. That's all. I'm sorry if I alarmed you. Everything's fine. I'm finished and am about to leave."

"Well, then, I'll just wait and see you home."

"There's no need, Sheriff. It's only to Mrs. Busby's."

"Yes, ma'am, I know that. But it's Saturday night, and the saloons are doin' a lot of business. Some brawls and worse bound to happen. Saturday night's no time for ladies to be out and about alone."

"That's very kind of you, but I'm sure I'll be perfectly all right."

"Well, if you don't mind, Miss McClaren. For my own peace of mind, I reckon I'd like to see you safely home." The gentle voice concealed the firm steel of resolve underneath.

Mindy realized there was no use to argue. Taylor was determined.

"Well, if you insist." Her tone was slightly exasperated. "I'll just finish up this copy and put it on Pete's desk to set on Monday. Then I'll be ready."

"You just take your time, Miss McClaren. I've got all night. Things don't get real rowdy until about eleven. But I'll be on duty till dawn anyway."

Mindy was actually amused rather than irritated by the big Texan's insistence. It was most thoughtful and considerate of him to be concerned about her welfare.

She put on her jacket and bonnet, and together they left the building. Mindy locked the door and, after a slight hesitation, took the arm Taylor offered her.

She had to admit there was something reassuring about being escorted by this tall, strong fellow. His commanding appearance alone would ward off any potential danger. As they passed the numerous saloons on the way to Mrs. Busby's, raucous music, loud voices, and occasional shouts emerged from the constantly opening and shutting swinging doors.

When they arrived at the boarding house door, Mindy slipped her hand from his arm. "Thank you very much, Sheriff."

"My pleasure," he replied solemnly. Then he added, "Miss McClaren, would you do me a favor?"

"Yes, of course, what is it?"

"Calling me 'Sheriff' seems kinda formal. How about callin' me by my first name, like we were friends."

Friendships formed fast in Coarse Gold, Mindy thought. The social prohibition of Woodhaven, where a lady wasn't called by her first name except by her relatives and a few close friends—and never by a gentleman unless they were engaged—didn't exist here.

"If you'd like me to—"

"I sure would."

"Well, goodnight, Taylor, and thanks again," Mindy said and went in the house, smiling to herself. She was impressed. This was a man physically strong and yet gentle. A man who probably needed to be tough, who had faced many dangerous situations, risked his life often, and faced vicious outlaws numerous times. Still there was something endearing about Sheriff—no, *Taylor*—Bradford. Something she hadn't given him credit for on first meeting. She must remember not to jump to conclusions about anyone. Especially here in Coarse Gold.

Chapter 14

The third week in October, the announcement of the Harvest Dance was brought to the paper. Contrary to the festival's name, very few farmers actually lived near Coarse Gold, but the inaccuracy didn't seem to bother anyone. This annual community party was a highly anticipated event.

"Kind of the last fling before the snow starts. Folks get pretty locked in then," Byron told Mindy as he gave her the handwritten copy to edit and give to Pete.

In the dining room at Mrs. Busby's boarding house, the closer the date of the dance drew, the more the subject was talked about at the table. There was a great deal of joshing back and forth, loud teasing about who any one of the miners might escort. Since there was a scarcity of young single women in Coarse Gold, Mindy was conscious of several hopeful glances in her direction. When the discussion became too personal, she would finished her meal and excuse herself before any direct invitation was posed.

As a matter of fact, Mindy had not planned to go at all until Byron told her that he expected her to cover it for the newspaper. There was no possibility of refusing the assignment.

"Everyone goes and everyone wants a mention in the write-up," he told her.

"Do you go?" she asked, trying to imagine him in a social situation.

"Of course. Wouldn't miss it. At least, I'll put in an appearance." He answered testily then went back to writing his editorial.

Timmy was the one who filled Mindy in on all the details. The dance was held in the storeroom above the general store. The wooden boxes were pushed back against the wall for the occasion to make room for a dance floor in the center. The floor was polished by dragging a heavy hay bale across the surface a number of times. The ladies of the town supplied pies and cakes, and as Timmy assured Mindy, there would be plenty of liquid refreshment.

Not unexpectedly, Taylor shyly asked Mindy if she would go to the dance with him.

"Thank you but I'm covering it for the paper, Taylor, so it will be more work for me than a social occasion."

He looked disappointed but said, "I reckon it'll be the same for me. Though I'll not be there in my official capacity, you just never know when I may be called on. When some of these fellas get to imbibin', there's no telling what high jinks they'll get up to."

"I'm glad you understand, Taylor. A job's a job."

He was flattered. Mindy thought he understood, though really, he didn't. At least about *her* job. He'd never known a woman who had any kind of work outside her home or who felt anything was more important than marriage or being a wife and mother. She was sure different from any of the females in his large Texas family, different from any of the girls he'd courted back home, and especially the type of woman he'd met since coming to Colorado. He was strongly attracted to Mindy McClaren, but he sure couldn't figure her out. And that made him pretty uncomfortable.

The night of the dance, Mindy walked down main street on her way to the general store. She heard loud music pouring out through the windows of the second story. Once she was inside, the sound was almost deafening. Provided by a tinny piano brought over from one of the saloons, a banjo, a fiddle and a set of drums, the music was vigorously if not skillfully played. Dancers were already whirling around, arms flailing, feet sliding enthusiastically, unconcerned even if not in step or in time to the tempo of their own energy.

A bar had been set up along one side. Cowboys, three deep, were lined up in front of it, all with one elbow on the shiny surface and their bodies half-turned to watch the dancers spinning, their boot toes tapping. Mindy wondered if they were getting up the courage to find a partner and try their own luck on the slippery dance floor. Probably most of them had never even danced before, or it had been such a long time ago, in another lifetime back east. Whatever their reason, they were fortifying themselves for the effort much as they might at the start of a long cattle drive.

Lest they should run out of strength or zest to keep playing their instruments, the band was kept constantly supplied with drinks. The numbers of bottles set beside their chairs on the platform from which they swigged between numbers, increased at an alarmingly fast rate.

Mindy could not help but compare this scene to the decorum of dancing parties in Woodhaven. There, everything was done according to an established order. Ladies were given dance cards on which gentlemen politely requested their names to be written, a favor bestowed genteelly. Chaperones, overseeing those dancers, would have dropped over in shock if any man had approached a girl with the salutation, "If you ain't spoken for, how about the next dance?" as was the common approach Mindy witnessed here.

Mindy moved around on the outskirts of the dance floor, nodding and speaking to the people she knew, making a few notes in the small notebook she pulled out of her pocket every once in a while to jot down a name in case she forgot it. She wasn't sure when she became aware of the sensation that she was being watched. As if somehow compelled, she involuntarily turned and met the intense stare of a man directly across the room.

He stood head and shoulders above the men standing near him. It wasn't just his height that made her notice him, however. The way he was dressed would have stood out in any crowd. He was wearing a well-cut gray broadcloth coat that reached the top of his black polished boots, a satin vest in a bold paisley design, an immaculate white ruffled shirt, and a black string tie. Apart from his attire, he was exceptionally fine looking. He had a magnificent head of wavy, chestnut brown hair. The eyes that held hers were dark but with a mischievous sparkle. While their gaze held, his mouth lifted in a slow smile—regarding her as if he already knew her. Mindy's cheeks flamed hotly under his knowing glance. She felt a strange sense of recognition. But of course that was impossible. He was a total stranger. She had never seen him in all the time she had been in Coarse Gold.

She started to turn away but suddenly was unable to move. The man was sauntering toward her with an assured stride. The next thing she knew he was right in front of her. He towered over her with that disarming smile.

"Good evening, Miss McClaren." His voice was deep with a kind of vibrancy that played on her nerve ends like the mellow sound of a cello.

"Good evening." Mindy wished she didn't sound so breathless.

"I haven't had the pleasure of being formally introduced, so I hope you'll forgive me my boldness approaching you. I'm Wade Carrigan."

His manners were such a contrast to the rough-hewn regulars Mindy had become used to, she was taken aback. Inexplicably, Mindy's heart somersaulted. It was insane. Instinctively Mindy knew that this man would be easy to fall in love with. And that would be dangerous.

"Would you care to dance?"

Actually Mindy had not planned to dance. She had only intended to "put in an appearance," as Byron had suggested, take her notes, and leave. But she couldn't resist this invitation.

Carrigan could dance—and he danced superbly. In his arms, Mindy glided easily, despite the wild music and the couples improvising around them.

As the tune came to an end she felt hot and very out of breath. Carrigan looked down at her and suggested they step outside for some fresh air. For a moment she hesitated. Was it wise to leave with someone she had just met?

However, the party had all the earmarks of getting more boisterous. The way both the musicians and guests were quaffing down the liquid refreshment, perhaps it was a good idea. As they made their way through the crowd Mindy felt the target of some resentful glances. Mainly from the men who were gearing up their nerve to ask the pretty newspaper lady for a dance. She caught Taylor's dismayed expression as she passed him. He momentarily broke off whatever he was saying to two pretty blondes, who both looked glad to see Mindy go.

Out of the corner of her eyes she saw Byron at the bar and wondered if she should stop and offer to accompany him home. But Carrigan's hand was guiding her firmly down the stairs and into the night.

Outside was cool and the dark sky full of stars. "This is certainly my lucky night," Carrigan remarked. "This party was a surprise, and meeting you a pleasanter one. I'm just back in town. Been up at my silver mine. Brought some samples down to be assayed. My partner's still there. It looks like we've struck a rich vein." He paused, "I didn't know there was a new reporter at the *Gazette* until someone pointed you out."

"I've only been here a few months," Mindy told him. "A lady reporter's quite a novelty in this part of the country. I take it you're from back east?"

It had been a long time since Mindy had been in the company of such an attractive man, who was evidently interested in getting to know her. In her nervousness, she heard herself rattle on about how excited she was to be here, how interesting she found the job, and how beautiful Colorado is. Finally realizing she was chattering like a magpie, she halted abruptly.

But Wade seemed to listen attentively. His eyes were fastened on her—not out of interest in what Mindy was saying, but because he was thinking how attractive she was. Compared to the usual women Coarse Gold offered, Miss McClaren was something entirely new. He enjoyed seeing how her eyes shone, how animated her expression, and how the light shining out from the windows above sent bronze glints on her auburn hair.

Realizing she had been going on and on while he said nothing, Mindy felt self-conscious. She took a few steps away, "I really must go."

"Home? This early?

"No, to the newspaper."

"Sure you don't want to go back in? Dance some more?" He sounded amused.

"I think not." In spite of herself her voice was regretful. "I like to write my reports up while everything is still fresh in my mind."

"I take it you're not a social butterfly?"

"No, I consider myself a working woman. Although that isn't to say I didn't enjoy the dance."

So did I, and I was looking forward to another, maybe several." He paused, "Any chance of seeing you again? Tomorrow maybe?"

"Tomorrow?" Mindy couldn't believe the way her heart was hammering.

Carrigan fell in step alongside her, and Mindy realized he intended to walk her back to the newspaper office.

Do you ride, Miss McClaren? He asked.

"Yes, I do but—"

"Good. I stable two horses at Flaherty's Livery. Would you like to ride into the hills tomorrow, have a picnic by the river?"

Mindy hesitated, "I haven't ridden since coming here."

"Well, not to worry. Both my mounts are gentle. You shouldn't have any trouble. I'll get the groom to side-saddle Sugarfoot. Shall I come for you at ten?"

"Ten would be fine—Oh, no, I almost forgot, tomorrow's Sunday. I won't be back from church until noon."

"Ah, yes, keeping the Sabbath. Of course, you would."

His tone was cool. Afraid he was about to withdraw his invitation, Mindy suggested, "You're welcome to attend. We could leave directly after service was over."

Wade gave a short laugh. "Thank you, but no thanks. It might upset the congregation too much to see me there. Not tomorrow anyway. Perhaps another time."

They had reached the newspaper building. Wade glanced at the darkened interior.

"Surely you're not going in there and work alone at this hour of the night?"

"Oh, yes, I often do. It's sometimes easier to work when everything is quiet. No one coming in to disturb my train of thought."

"Are you able to manage your train of thought so neatly, Miss McClaren? I'm impressed. I find my own thoughts run amok at times, and I have no control over them at all. As well as my feelings. They are the hardest to keep on a tight rein."

Mindy heard the innuendo in his words that would be risky to explore, "Well, thank you, Mr. Carrigan for escorting me."

Wade put out his hand on her arm to detain her. "Wait, please. Where do I come for you tomorrow?"

"I board at Mrs. Busby's."

"Aha, the doyen of landladies," he chuckled. "My calling for you there should start the rumor mill humming."

"Would you rather I meet you somewhere else?"

"No not at all, Miss McClaren. I am always delighted to give the town something to gossip about." Wade laughed then placed his hand under her elbow and escorted her right to the door. "This has been a most happy chance, Miss McClaren. I look forward to tomorrow with great pleasure."

Chapter 15

*M*indy stirred restlessly in the pew. The sermon this Sunday seemed interminably long. Her thoughts kept straying to the fascinating man she had met the night before, Wade Carrigan. She was also uncomfortably conscious of the fact she had worn her best bonnet to church and that the hat pins securing it were jabbing her scalp. Well, soon she would be rid of both the hat and her tightly laced corset.

She was really looking forward to being on horseback again. She had never owned a formal riding habit, but her denim skirt, and jacket in a becoming blue, should be suitable for the ride into the hills. She would wear the broad-brimmed Goucho hat with its leather chinstrap and tie a scarf around her neck.

Suddenly the minister's voice reached her distracted ears. The Scripture he was using to base his message seemed directed at her own preoccupation with appearance. Matthew 6:28: "Consider the lilies of the field, they do not toil, neither do they spin, and yet Solomon in all his glory was not clothed as one of these. Therefore do not worry saying, 'What shall we wear? What shall we put on?' for after all these things the Gentiles seek. Seek first the kingdom of God. . . ." Convicted, Mindy sat up straighter. Instead of listening she'd been concerned with how she would look to a perfect stranger.

For the next half-hour she tried to concentrate on what Reverend Thompson was saying. Afterward, she hurried back to the boarding house to change.

As she came out to the hallway on her way to wait for Wade on the front porch, she ran into Mrs. Busby. "Coming in to dinner? I've got your favorite apricot cobbler for dessert."

"Not today, Mrs. Busby. Actually, I'm going on a picnic with Wade Carrigan."

Mrs. Busby gasped "A picnic? With Wade Carrigan? Surely not alone?"

"Why, yes, Mrs. Busby, why ever not?"

Usually not easily surprised, Mrs. Busby seemed flustered. "I know you're new in town and not expected to know everything—but it's just that Wade Carrigan has a well-known reputation for being a lady's man, to put it mildly. Certainly not *your* type of gentleman, dearie."

Mindy had become used to Mrs. Busby's take-charge attitude to everyone under her roof. But this seemed a little much. After all, she was a grown woman, on her own, making her own living, certainly capable of good judgment in choosing friends.

She didn't appreciate this unsolicited advice. Mainly because it triggered a little unease on her own part of having accepted Wade's invitation on such short acquaintance. But she couldn't back out now. First, because it make her seem unsure and immature. "He seems perfectly gentlemanly to *me*, Mrs. Busby."

Mrs. Busby looked a little chagrined as if she realized she may have overstepped her place. She pursed her mouth as if to say more then decided to let well enough alone. She gave Mindy a "don't say I didn't warn you" look and murmured, "A word to the wise is sufficient" as she went to ring the dinner bell with more than usual vigor.

Wade was waiting outside, with two horses. He helped Mindy up onto the one with the side saddle, then mounted the other, "Well, we're off." Mindy turned her horse, and together they walked them down the dusty Main Street. Mindy imagined not only Mrs. Busby's sharp eyes following their progress, but many other curious pairs as well.

The river was about four miles out of town.I It wasn't a river, really, but just a dry narrow path fed by the spring melt and lined with willow trees. That day it seemed to have a magic all its own. The autumn haze softened the landscape, the sounds, and the very wind that gently stirred the aspen trees in the grove Wade chose for their picnic.

The ride out from town made them hungry for the picnic lunch of ham, cheese, hard-boiled eggs, apple tarts, bottled lemonade, and root beer. Afterward, they walked along what would have been the riverbed after a summer cloudburst. Mindy was becoming accustomed to the starkness of the Colorado landscape yet found in it a beauty untarnished by expectancy. It was new and different from the lush green of the countryside where she had grown up but that made it even more interesting.

She did most of the talking. Wade's attentiveness encouraged her to tell him more about herself than she had told anyone since coming west. She told him about some of the things she had written, the articles on women's education, the features she had done in the Dixie Dillon column. This especially amused him. He threw back his head and laughed heartily when she recounted some of the letters and some of her replies. "So you give advice to the lovelorn, Miss McClaren. I shall have to remember that if ever I'm smitten."

The fact that she could amuse him and receive such undivided attention was flattering. Since going to work at the *Gazette,* Mindy had worked such long hours that she had almost forgotten what fun a carefree outing could be. She found Wade utterly charming and not a bit threatening, as Mrs. Busby had intimated. As the shadows began to lengthen, she was sorry to see their wonderful time together come to an end. She had enjoyed the ride, the picnic, and the fun and pleasure of a delightful companion. They rode back into town at dusk and parted at the boarding house steps.

Mindy did not want to join the rest of the boarders for supper. She slipped past the dining room, where the sounds of clanking plates, water being poured into tumblers, and the rattle of silverware mingled with voices and laughter. She didn't want to meet Mrs. Busby's disapproving glance nor have the day she had enjoyed spoiled by questions or explanations.

That night she slept soundly, awakened later than usual. She had to hurry to get to work. When she arrived, however, the newspaper office was still locked. Timmy, who did not have a key, was sitting dejectedly on the steps. It seems Karr had not shown up—unusual for a man who often worked with a hangover on Mondays. Upon checking, Mindy discovered that starting Saturday night of the Harvest party he had gone on a longer, worse binge over the weekend and was sleeping it off.

Karr didn't come in until late Tuesday afternoon. Although apologetic, he was unable to do much work. Mindy suspected from his frequent trips over to the Golden Slipper that he was trying the legendary but untrue remedy of 'the hair of the dog that bit you.'

Mindy gathered together the main stories for the week and wrote a glowing report of the Community Harvest Dance, filling in some of the gaps of information she had missed by leaving early with Wade Carrigan. On Wednesday afternoon, with the paper almost ready to "be put to bed," Mindy chanced to look up from her desk and saw Wade enter the newsroom. She had been so busy taking over Byron's work she had hardly time to recall the day they had spent together.

As Wade approached her desk her heart gave a little flip-flop. His eyes darkly mischievous, he told her, "I've got the horses saddled and ready to ride."

She would have liked nothing better than to say yes, to jump up from her desk, and run hand-in-hand with him out of the grubby newsroom, away from the smell of print-er's ink and the clunk of the old press, to ride with the cool wind in her face out to where the jagged blue line of the hills met the sky.

Regretfully, she turned him down. She still had a few items to finish so that all the copy would be ready for Pete to set. "I'll have to work into the evening to make sure all the deadlines are met."

Wade seemed reluctant to accept her refusal.

"You're sure I can't tempt you?"

Mindy shook her head. She couldn't depend on Byron. "Sorry. I really can't. Karr is—well, not feeling well. It's up to me to get the paper out."

"You're a woman of discipline, aren't you?" She couldn't tell if Wade was mocking her or if there was a note of admiration or something else in his tone.

"I just try to be responsible. People expect the paper will be out tomorrow."

"Karr doesn't seem to care."

"But he does!" Mindy rose quickly to the editor's defense. "It's just that he has this—problem, sometimes.

A strange expression passed swiftly across Wade's face.

"Are you always so understanding about other people's weaknesses, their faults?"

Not wanting to seem sanctimonious, Mindy stammered a little, replying, "I try to be. I have enough failings of my own to be tolerant of someone else's."

"'He who casts the first stone,' right?" Wade said sardonically, raising his eyebrows. "The Christian virtues of compassion and forgiveness."

She was surprised at his quoting Scripture. It seemed out of character somehow. But then she reminded herself she did not know Wade Carrigan all that well.

"Aren't we all supposed to be?"

"If we live by those rules."

For a moment Mindy saw something in Wade's eyes that troubled her. A darkness. Melancholy? Before she could discern what it was, he smiled.

"Well, if I can't lead you astray, I'll go." He walked to the door, then turned back to say, "I'll be thinking of you grubbing here while I'm out enjoying the great outdoors."

He left and she struggled to get back to work. Their enigmatic exchange kept cropping up in her mind. Wade Carrigan was more than a handsome façade. There were layers and layers within him that would be fascinating to unravel.

It was late when she finally got up from her desk, stretched her aching muscles, picked up her jacket, and blew out the lamp. She made her way across the room to the door, went out, and locked it behind her.

"All done?" a deep male voice asked. Startled Mindy spun around practically into Wade Carrigan's arms.

"What are you doing here?"

"Waiting for you. Come on, I'll walk you home."

At one point, as they chatted about this and that on the way to Mrs. Busby's, Mindy was aware of a spicy smell, the hint of tobacco and fresh linen. For a moment, she felt almost dizzy and quickly moved away. But it was too late; he had already reached out, circled her upper arms with his strong hands, and pulled her close. Before she knew it, he was kissing her as she had never before been kissed. Not possessively nor passionately, but with an assurance that was more unsettling—as if he knew she wanted to be kissed.

When she could breathe again, she drew back, looked up at him. Wade spoke softly, "I've wanted to do that since

Sunday. I didn't dare. I was afraid I'd scare you off. Now I'm not so sure that would happen. You are some lady, Miss McClaren. I have an idea you don't scare easily."

Later, that night, Mindy lay in bed, wide awake, the memory of his kiss still vivid. Her cheeks warmed as she remembered how she had responded. That had never happened with Judson, the only other man whom she had ever kissed. And they were practically engaged at the time.

She never intended for something like this to happen. Falling in love wasn't in her plan. Being in love made a woman vulnerable, dependent. She had come out west to avoid that. To reach her own goals, realize her own dreams. Falling in love with a man like Wade Carrigan could be a disaster for someone like herself. He was unlike any other men she had known; her father, her brothers, Farell Judson, who lived by the established code of ethics. Wade sauntered through life making his own rules.

While his difference made him fascinating to her, Mindy wondered what he had seen in *her*? She tried to remember just what they had talked about the day of the picnic. He seemed to like hearing about her, about her hometown, her family, and he especially liked to hear about her relatives— the odd names of the various ones amused him.

"What about your name?" he had asked. "Mindy must be short for something. Minerva? Minetta?"

"You'd never guess," she said, then explained about Farell's stammer. "My brother couldn't pronounce my real name, so I became Mindy."

"So what is it then? I'm curious."

"Independence."

Wade looked amused. "Independence! That figures. It suits you." It occurred to Mindy that, although she had told him practically her whole life story, she had not learned much about him. Wade talked little about himself. When Mindy tried to probe gently about his background— how, when, and why he'd come to Coarse Gold—Wade

118

deftly changed the subject. "I have a checkered past you wouldn't want to know about."

During the next week, Mindy moved like a person drifting in a cloud. She found Wade irresistible. A reporter learned to look beneath the surface, to observe people, ferret out the motives for their behavior and actions. But with Wade she drew a blank. She knew there must be more to his character hidden beneath the smooth, self-assured façade. She had seen beneath Judson's mother's refined veneer to discover that she had a fishwife's temper and vocabulary. She recalled telling Wade about the incident at the Powells' anniversary party and how it had pulled the scales from her eyes to see a horrid, mean-spirited personality revealed. "Things were certainly not what they seemed."

"Things seldom are, Mindy," Wade had replied with unusual seriousness.

In the days that followed Mindy was happy just being with him. That was enough for now. Maybe when they got to know each other better, she would find out about his life before Coarse Gold of which Wade gave her no clue. His tender, teasing manner warded off inquiry and Mindy was too enraptured to pursue it. She left her reportorial skills at the office when she was with Wade.

On Monday of the second week, Mindy woke up after a lovely dream. She lay there for a few minutes smiling. Of course, Wade was in it. But the dream was not even as pleasurable as the reality.

She and Wade had spent almost the entire weekend together. She felt guilty about it skipping church because Wade suggested they ride out early and watch the sunrise together. "I must be stronger, not give into his whims so much," she told herself half-heartedly as she got dressed. These days she spent more time fixing her hair and choosing her wardrobe—in case she were to see Wade. He dropped by the newspaper any time of the day. She never knew exactly when. Funny, she used to not care how she looked because she was always in a hurry to get to the newspaper. Lately she had been meeting Wade for breakfast at the Palace Hotel, where Wade was staying. Mindy hummed happily as she buttoned the white ruffled blouse and slipped on the blue jacket that nipped her waist above the flaring darker blue skirt. A quick check in the mirror showed her a little pale with faint lavender shadows under her eyes from keeping such late hours. Wade never wanted to say goodnight and they lingered long over parting. In spite of the pallor, there was something new and shining about her. She had the look of someone who had been told she was lovely and had recently been often and thoroughly kissed.

Her step was light as she crossed Main Street, went up the steps of the Palace Hotel, and walked into the dining room. Only a few people were there. The table Wade usually occupied by the window was empty. Maybe, he hadn't come down yet. Mindy turned and looked expectantly toward the staircase, imagining that any minute Wade would descend, freshly shaved, groomed, his suit pressed, boots polished, and linen spotless. But he was nowhere to be seen. The clerk behind the desk was reading, a penny dreadful with a lurid cover of a cowboy shoot-out. Mindy did not want to ask him about Wade or show undue interest in him. The lobby of the Palace was a hotbed of gossip. That the woman newspaper reporter was inquiring of the whereabouts of the dashing Wade Carrigan would make a juicy morsel to pass from ear to ear. So, instead, Mindy waited until Bertha, the waitress she knew, emerged from the kitchen with a large platter of scrambled eggs and sausage. After Bertha had set it down on a nearby table, she saw Mindy, nodded, came over to her, wiping her hands on her blue checked apron.

"Mornin', Miss McClaren, what'll it be—hotcakes or muffins?"

"Just some coffee, please, Bertha."

120

"That ain't enough to keep a bird alive. You ought to have a stack and some bacon, mebbe?"

"Thanks, Bertha. But that will be enough for now." Then as casually as she could manage, Mindy asked. "Has Mr. Carrigan had breakfast yet?" In spite of herself, she felt a blush rising into her cheeks.

Bertha, busy wiping the oil-cloth cover on a nearby table, answered, "Oh, he come down early. Jest as we was opening the kitchen. Had his usual ham and eggs. Then he rode off. He'd left orders at the stables last night to have his horse ready, and we packed his saddle bags with enough grub for a long ride. I 'spect he's gone out to his mine."

Gone? Without a word? Without even a mention of it the night before? After the way he'd kissed her? Mindy's face flamed. Why hadn't he said anything about leaving? She had a hard time concealing her shock. She took a sip of the coffee Bertha poured for her.

She should have known better. It was her own fault she was hurt. She had allowed Wade Carrigan entry into a heart she had thought protected. A deep sense of betrayal trembled all through her. She got up, left the dining room, went back across the street to the boarding house, and back into her room. She was shivering uncontrollably. She would have to pull herself together before going into the paper. And she better start working on forgetting Wade Carrigan.

Chapter 16

*A*s if to match her downcast mood, the weather turned gray. October's beautiful blue skies became heavy with clouds, and it rained steadily.

In the wake of Wade's sudden, unexplained departure, Mindy struggled to deal with her heartache by throwing herself into her work. She should never have let it happen. For a few short weeks, she had let herself be diverted from her goals of becoming a topnotch newspaper journalist. She despised her own weakness for falling in love so easily and so hard with a man she hardly knew.

In spite of her decision to forget him, she kept thinking over the events of their time together, wondering if it was something she had said or done that had made him wary. In spite of his obvious attraction to her, Wade had never once said the words she longed to hear: "I love you." Was the romance all in her imagination?

Mindy was sure Byron had observed her preoccupation with Wade. He often took his meals at the Palace and had seen the two of them eating dinner together, sometimes breakfast. He couldn't miss Wade showing up at the newspaper office, and then notice that Mindy would hurriedly clear her desk and leave with him. He'd made no comment, but Mindy was aware of the calculating glances he had given her when he caught her daydreaming over her work.

Mindy determined to stop thinking about Wade. She would concentrate on carving a niche for herself at the *Gazette*, make a name for herself in journalism. She searched for an idea for an article of local interest told from a woman's viewpoint.

In a conversation with Mrs. Busby, the seed for one was planted. Quickly, Mindy outlined the idea to Byron. He leaned back in his swivel chair; a smile tugged at the corners of his mouth. "So you're back to being a real newspaper woman, are you?"

Mindy blushed but lifted her chin defensively. "I'm always that, always looking for a good story, wherever it is, whoever may have it."

"Uh-huh." Byron's eyes were amused, "So what is it this time, McClaren?"

"Mrs. Busby told me there's a really old lady, Bedelia Warren, who as a child came west with her family on a wagon train. They got caught by weather before the Rockies and decided to camp near there instead of going on, to wait until spring to cross the mountains. Well, it seems they were ambushed by Apaches and the little girl was kidnapped." She paused. "She was held hostage but eventually escaped and made her way back. A hazardous adventure. That's the story I'd like to write. Mrs. Busby says only a few people know about it. It would make a great feature for the paper. I also think it might sell to one of the eastern periodicals. They are always interested in anything western. And a first-person account of such a dramatic event . . . well, it would be—"

"You would write it, of course, not just take down her words?"

"Yes, I would. The way I did those two pieces I showed you from my Dixie Dillon column. 'Bedelia Warren as told to I. Howard McClaren.'" She waited, "So what do you think?"

"Great idea. Do it! We'll print it."

"Thanks, Byron, thank you." Mindy jumped up and was almost tempted to give him a hug, but he was scowling as if he anticipated such a move, so she resisted.

Bedelia Warren's story was a success. Everyone commented on it when it appeared in the *Gazette*. Mrs. Warren became the recipient of much adulation, visits, gifts of food and flowers, in admiration for her bravery. Much to Mindy's delight, the old lady thoroughly enjoyed her new celebrity.

Byron was pleased, she could tell. More and more he treated her as his peer. He was unstinting in his praise when he liked something she'd written. He left books and notes on her desk and encouraged her by pointing out possible subjects for future columns. Often, when she was about to leave for the day, he would call her over to his desk to share something he'd read or thought she'd find interesting.

Since he was currently on the wagon, Mindy decided that staying late, drinking mug after mug of coffee together, listening to his stories of his days on a big city daily newspaper, might be helpful in keeping him out of the local saloons. Besides she was learning a great deal about the newspaper business from him. She also knew Byron was a terribly lonely person. Why else would he be in this far away desert town alone? What had he left behind? From his stories, she gathered he once held a top job on an important eastern newspaper. He never bragged about it, but it was not hard to tell he had covered some of the biggest stories of the last fifteen years.

Busy with her work Mindy managed to think less about the unhappy ending to her short romance with Wade Carrigan.

November was bleak and blustery. Cold, freezing winds and rain pelted the town. Everyone complained how miserable the weather was. One day Timmy, drenched to the bone, came back from the post office with the mail. He stood at the door dripping water, wrung out his cap, and shook back his hair from his freckled face. Mindy poured him a cup of steaming coffee and handed it to him as he dumped her mail on her desk.

"Better take your boots off and hang your jacket near the stove to dry out," she suggested as she looked through the sheaf of letters. Then, one letter with a familiar handwriting caught her eye. The postmark was Woodhaven. She was aware that Timmy had asked her something and that she answered, not knowing what either the question or answer was. She sat down and opened the letter—from Judson.

Dear Mindy,

Don't be mad, but I begged your Aunt Jen for your address. She was hard to persuade. She said, "If Mindy wanted you to have it, she'd have given it to you." That's true, but it doesn't make it any easier to take. I don't have your way with words, but what I'm writing comes from the heart. Mindy, I'm sorry how everything turned out for us. I didn't want it to end. I still love you, and I wish things could have been different.

I'm taking the chance that maybe you've thought things over, and maybe—just maybe—you're sorry too. If you've changed your mind, I would come to Colorado and bring you home, where you belong and where things would work out. If we'd both try, I think they would. I know I would really try to understand about your writing. Why not give it a second chance?

Always yours,
Judson

Mindy put the single page back in its envelope. It was funny that this letter should reach her now. A few weeks ago when she was feeling so downhearted over Wade Carrigan, before she got her second wind with the writing of the Bedelia Warren story, Judson's appeal might have moved her.

She knew he was sincere. But she also knew he really hadn't changed his attitude about her being a journalist. She could read between the lines. He hoped that if she came back to Woodhaven, gradually her ambition would fade. Once married, Judson must believe, their home and, eventually perhaps, their children would be her priority.

Slowly, Mindy tore the letter into tiny pieces and tossed them into the big wastepaper basket by her desk. There was no point in answering it. That part of her life was over. Mindy drew a blank piece of paper from her IN basket and began to compose a piece for the special Thanksgiving Day edition.

After a hectic afternoon putting the paper to bed, an especially frantic time for everyone due to the flood of ads received at the eleventh hour, Mindy and Byron were sharing a cup of coffee and waiting for the first paper off the press so they could see the results of all their hard work.

Suddenly, Mindy noticed Byron's expression change. She turned to follow the direction he was looking and saw Taylor come into the building, his right arm in a sling. The brawny lawman looked unusually pale and gaunt.

"What happened to you?" Byron asked, setting down his mug. Mindy gasped, "Taylor, come sit down."

"Shoot-out over at Silver Creek," Taylor said as he walked over to Byron and slumped down in the chair opposite his cluttered desk. "Bank robbery. Gang of about four. I was just ridin' through when it happened. I saw them coming out of the bank. They was caught as red-handed as you could want, carrying bags of money right out there in broad daylight. Soon as I saw what was going on, I drew my gun and hollered, 'Halt!' They run for their horses and started mountin'. I aimed and started shootin'—I knowed I got one in the leg for he let out a yell and grabbed his thigh. His horse wheeled around but he hung onto the bridle and pulled hisself up by the reins. I shot again but one of his partners turned, saw me, and shot. Hit my gun arm. Bullet lodged right above my wrist and shattered the bone so's I dropped my gun. I'd 've given chase otherwise, but they gave their horses their heads and were off. The local deputy came piling out of the store 'crost the street, wavin' his pistol and shootin' every whichaway, but it didn't do no good. Durned if they didn't get away." He shook his head disconsolately. "Cleaned out the bank. The stage had just delivered the payroll for the mine."

"Any idea who they were?" asked Byron eager for more details so he could write it up for page one, next edition. Or maybe even for an EXTRA if the story warranted.

"Not for sure. But I got a good enough idea. There's been a rash of bank robberies. Same outfit. Bad bunch, but mighty clever. This didn't seem like their usual operation. They're pretty smooth. Come in like a customer, well-dressed, nice mannered, then slip a note to the teller, and 'fore anyone knows it, they've bagged the money and made off. Don't even fire a shot. Doggone it—'scuse me, Miss Mindy." Taylor nodded in her direction. "I'd sure have liked to nab 'em, bring 'em in. They're a menace to the hard-working folks around here. Those miners whose pay they got work long and hard and to be cheated out of it—"

"Well, four against one. You couldn't have fought them all," Byron commented.

"Taylor, you might have been killed," added Mindy.

"Nah," Taylor lifted his bandaged arm. "No way. I could've took at least two of them 'fore the others made off if I hadn't been taken by surprise. I should've protected myself better." He sighed heavily. "But anyway that one fella was bleedin' like a stuck pig, left a trail of blood—he'll have to stop have that leg fixed somewhere by some doctor or he'll lose it."

Her eyes full of admiration Mindy said, "I think you were very brave, Taylor."

Taylor flushed and looked embarrassed but pleased.

"Well, let's all go over to Mrs. Busby's and have a good dinner while Taylor tells us more about his adventure," suggested Byron. He bent and dragged a big, shabby umbrella from under his desk. "What do you say?"

"Sounds good to me." Taylor looked hopefully at Mindy who also agreed.

When Mrs. Busby saw Taylor's sling, she was all concern and sympathy. She gave them her best table and served them buffalo steaks, roasted potatoes and turnips, and carrots in a rich gravy. She hovered over them until she assured herself that three of her favorite people were well fed and enjoying everything. Mindy had to cut Taylor's meat for him, which amused Byron and tickled Taylor no end.

After Mrs. Busby brought them custard pie and Byron had polished off his, he stood up, "I'm going to leave you two young people now, got to take care of a few things. Thanks for the good story, Taylor. When we've got it ready to set, come by and check all the facts. The *Gazette*'s motto is 'The truth, nothing but the truth,' in its articles."

Left by themselves, Taylor looked uncomfortable. "I hope he don't make it sound like one of them wild western tales."

"He won't. Byron's a professional. Sticks strictly to facts. Anyway, the truth is you *are* a hero, Taylor. People should know what a brave, courageous lawman they have here."

Taylor smiled. Coming from Mindy those words meant a great deal. Then he frowned. "It makes me madder than a hornet when outlaws feed on other people's lives and work like that. They're smart enough to figger out ways to cheat and steal, why can't they use the same brains to earn an honest living?"

Mindy shrugged. "The world's made up of a lot of different kinds. There's no accounting for it."

"Well, as soon as my arm's healed, I'm goin' after them. I seen their faces, two of them anyway. They outsmarted themselves this time by not wearing masks or bandanas tied around their faces like most thieves do. I got a good look at the one I shot and the fella who shot me. The wounded one couldn't have got too far with that leg, had to stop somewhere, hole up until it's better." Taylor's mouth tightened determinedly. "I mean it, Mindy, I'm going to get that fella and his whole gang, bring 'em to justice."

They finished their coffee, and Taylor walked to Mindy's room door with her.

"Thanks for . . ." He reddened and smiled sheepishly. ". . . cuttin' my steak for me."

"The least I could do for a real hero. Well, try to get some rest and not dream about catching bank robbers."

"I can think of a whole lot of nicer things to dream about." He looked down at her. She was such a pretty little thing, he'd sure like to kiss her goodnight but . . .

"Goodnight, Taylor. Remember to come by the newspaper and check Byron's story before we go to press."

Taylor stood outside for a minute after Mindy had gone in and closed the door. He wished he'd had the gumption to at least ask her to go to the church social with him Sunday night.

Maybe he'd get the chance when he stopped by the paper tomorrow.

Chapter 17

*I*n December, Mindy worried that she might feel terribly blue on her first Christmas so far from home. But things were so busy at the paper that she hardly had time to be sad. They were putting out two additional pages of advertising by local businesses, as well as for announcements of special holiday events from schools, churches, and social clubs. One of the biggest events of the season would be a community party after the Christmas program at the town hall.

Early in the month a large package arrived for Mindy from North Carolina. When she went to the train station to pick it up, she saw it was a little worse for wear after its long journey. Although the words "DO NOT OPEN UNTIL CHRISTMAS DAY" were clearly printed on top, Mindy undid the outer wrapping, which was already quite tattered. She calculated the time difference between North Carolina and Colorado and decided she would be justified in opening her presents on eastern time.

Her conscience fought with her curiosity—and lost. So two days before Christmas Mindy opened the rest of the box. A sweet scent rose from one small, square box. A tag, written in her mother's fine Spencerian handwriting, identified it as "Roses from a Southern Garden." She was sure it contained potpourri, which her mother was an expert in making. It would be lovely to scatter the dried rose petals in her bureau drawer among her camisoles, chemises, and petticoats. The present from Farell was flat and square. His attached letter confirmed what she had suspected. A hand-bound book of his poetry:

> These are my newest poems. Inspiration is all around me here in this quiet, peaceful setting. I am sitting outside, a gentle wind blows the leafy branches overhead, and a bird is singing in the far meadow. My pen seems to flow more easily in these harmonious surroundings. The only thing that would make it complete is if you were here to listen to my poetry. I hope you will enjoy these and try to imagine the scene in which they were written.
> Ever your devoted brother,
> Farell

Mindy could not help shedding a few tears. She missed her brother—the hours spent together, confiding her heart and listening to him read his poetry. Now someone else, Miss Louella Asbury, Farell's new step-sister, was doing this with him. Grateful as she was that Farell had found such a sympathetic companion, she also felt a wee bit envious.

The other present from her mother was a needlepoint pillow containing crushed Balsam needles. It gave off the piney scent of the woods where the Asbury farm was located. Her mother had stitched russet pinecones on a dark green background and the words "Sweet Dreams" on the cover.

She had several other packages to open. One, from Tom and Emily, contained a picture of the three of them with their baby, Mindy's little niece, Melvina, whom she had never seen. Her brother Eph, still at the army post in Florida, sent an Indian woven sweetgrass basket she could use for sewing and odds and ends. Two more packages came from Woodhaven. First she opened the one from her favorite Aunt Sassy, a skilled needlewoman. It was a red velvet vest exquisitely embroidered with vines and leaves and tiny flowers.

The other gift was from Aunt Jen, a lovely "fascinator" knitted of delicate white wool. The very thing for wearing over her hair on cold evenings. As she drew it from the box and shook it out to try it on, an envelope fell out from the folds. Mindy picked it up and slit it open. Enclosed was a short note and a folded newspaper clipping. "Thought you'd be interested to see this." Aunt Jen had written on the margin. "TWO LOCAL FAMILIES JOINED IN MARRIAGE," the headline read. "The wedding of Anne Willoughby and Judson Powell took place in Grace Presbyterian Church on November 12ᵗʰ, a reception was held at the groom's parents' home—" Mindy skimmed the rest of the account.

Mindy drew a long breath. Judson married. Of course, Anne Willoughby had always fancied him. Anne had always been jealous that he so obviously preferred Mindy. *Well, I had my chance,* Mindy thought. She recalled Judson's letter, begging her to come home and offering to bring her back home just a short time ago. Well, broken hearts heal faster than people think.

Mindy crumpled up the clipping. It wasn't regret she felt, just the closing of one more chapter of her life back east. Now, she had a whole new life out here. She meant to enjoy it and Christmas. As she got dressed to attend the Christmas program and the community party that followed, Mindy felt an odd excitement. Although she was expected to do write-ups on both events for the *Gazette,* she felt the same kind of anticipation she used to have getting ready for a social event in Woodhaven. The new red-velvet vest, worn with a white ruffled blouse and a flared black taffeta skirt, was the perfect outfit for a holiday party.

Instead of pulling her hair back into its usual utilitarian knot, Mindy had brushed it up, caught it with a marquisette comb, then let it fall in a swirl of waves to her shoulders. She wound the pretty fascinator over her head and surveyed the effect in the mirror with satisfaction.

It was only a short walk from the boarding house to town hall, but because it had snowed the day before, she pulled on sturdy boots. She carried along dancing shoes for later. Even though she was officially "on assignment," Taylor had made her promise to save some dances for him. His arm was much improved although still stiff and awkward.

As she came out into the dark evening, Mindy looked up into the sky, where thousands of stars seemed to sparkle. The snow covering the ground seemed to reflect the light shining out from the windows of houses along the way.

Close to the town hall she heard voices singing "Joy to the World Various groups were on the program and must be rehearsing in the basement rooms.

Laughter and greetings floated on the crisply cold air as people, coming from all directions, met at the bottom of the town hall steps. They chatted while stomping their boots of snow before entering the building.

A magnificent tree was set upon the platform where the city council usually sat. School children had done most of the decorations. Strings of popcorn and red and green paper chains mingled with festoons of bright cranberry beads, striped peppermint candy canes, gilt angels, and silver stars. From interviewing the decorating chairwoman, Mindy found out that lighted candles on the branches had been considered but rejected. The fire marshal had pronounced the danger of fire too hazardous in a crowded place. Instead, tall red tapers had been placed on each window sill along both sides of the hall and burned brightly, giving both scent and glowing light to the otherwise cavernous interior.

A pianist and two of the musicians who played so riotously for the Harvest Dance, now looking starched and solemn in this setting, provided the musical background for the community carols sung with enthusiasm if not in perfect harmony. The Reverend Thompson took center stage, ascending the steps with as much authority and dignity as he usually did in the pulpit. The sounds of neighbors greeting neighbors and the shrill exclamations of excited children gradually hushed. He waited until the hall was quiet, then he greeted everyone with his usual, "Praise the Lord. I'll be taking my text from the gospel of Luke." He began to read, "'And it came to pass, in those days, a decree went out from Caesar that the whole world should be enrolled . . .'"

Listening, Mindy's heart traveled back across the years and miles to the first Christmas she could remember. Her parents had taken her to a Christmas service much like this one. She remembered the trip in the wagon, the wheels and horses hooves making sharp crunching sounds on the thin crust of the snow. The smell of cedar and candle wax pungent in the warmth of the church. She recalled sitting in her father's lap, conscious of the new crimson velvet dress she was wearing. The memory was so real she could almost feel his coat lapels against her cheek as she leaned her head on his broad shoulders during the choir's rendering of "Away in a Manger." As a child, Mindy had felt sad at the words "no crib for his head," imagining "the Little Lord Jesus, asleep in the hay." Even at that early age she had been sensitive to others' pain.

Christmas always brought back nostalgic memories, and this Christmas was no exception. As she watched the younger children take their places to sing "O Little Town of Bethlehem," she felt deeply moved. So caught up in the moment, she hardly noticed a kind of stirring at the end of her pew. Suddenly, she caught a whiff of a familiar cologne and turned her head to see who had just sat down beside her.

"Surprised?" Wade whispered.

Surprised and *thrilled. Yes!* but she was still hurt and angry that he had gone so abruptly without telling her, leaving her wondering about their relationship, what it had meant, or if it had meant anything. Even while Mindy tried to maintain her composure, joy surged through her. Wade slipped his hand over hers and pressed it. Dizzy with excitement, Mindy looked away and stared straight ahead, afraid her overflowing emotions would show. Everything around her seemed to become blurred, the shiny ornaments on the Christmas tree, the candles. All she was conscious of was Wade's presence and her own soaring happiness.

The party that followed was mainly for the youngsters. Frank Owensby, the blacksmith, a huge, genial man, played Santa Claus to the delight of the children and the hilarity of the adults. Presents and bags of hard candy were handed out. Punch and cakes and pies of many kinds were in abundant supply for refreshment.

With so much chatter and confusion, shrieks from the children, laughter from the adults, there wasn't a chance for Mindy and Wade to talk. She was filled with curiosity about where he had been and why he had left and came back so unexpectedly. She thought she had successfully overcome her disappointment and had gotten over her heartache at his seeming indifference. But now she was trembling with gladness that he was here. There would be time later to talk, to ask questions, to find the answers to the questions she'd asked herself over and over about Wade Carrigan. But underneath, she was not really sure she would get them.

Everything around her was seen as through a haze of happiness. She spoke to people she knew but could not call them by name. She accepted holiday wishes and gave them but could not remember what she had said. Through the clusters of chattering folks, she saw Taylor's tall figure moving toward her.

With a pang of dismay, she recalled how they had spoken earlier, of the dances he had requested and promises she had made. He was smiling widely as he approached. His eyes were focused on Mindy; he didn't seem to see Wade standing at a little distance behind her.

"Never saw you look so pretty, Miss Mindy. I been waiting all evenin' to tell you so."

"Thank you, Taylor." Mindy darted a quick look over her shoulder to check if Wade could overhear them.

"Dr. MacAvey checked my arm today. See, I can lift and move it just fine." He demonstrated. "So I'm looking forward to our dances. Can I get you some punch while they're tuning up?"

"Sorry, old boy." Wade stepped up alongside Mindy. "All Miss McClaren's dances are taken."

Taylor's face flushed a deep red. He glanced from Wade to Mindy then back to Wade. He looked confused. "I'm Taylor Bradford. *Sheriff* Bradford. Don't think I've had the pleasure."

Wade stuck out his hand. "Wade Carrigan. No title, just Wade." There was subtle sarcasm underneath the smooth voice. "Miss McClaren came with me and is leaving with me. In fact, we were just about to go, weren't we?" he smiled complacently. "Afraid the party's over, Sheriff."

Mindy started to say something. Wade was being deliberately condescending, making fun of Taylor. It was rude and unkind, but she didn't have a chance to amend it. Wade had taken her arm and was propelling her away from Taylor toward the door.

"Come along, Mindy." He placed a hand on her waist in an obvious gesture of possession. "Good night, Sheriff."

Outside in the frosty starlight, Mindy remonstrated, "Wade, you didn't need to be so—"

"What? Proprietary? That young man was about to steal you away. I couldn't allow that. Especially since, like one of the three wise men, 'I've traveled plains and mountains, fields and fountains' to reach you, to spend Christmas with you."

Just then a group of people came by, calling out "Merry Christmas" to Mindy, and she returned the wishes. She still felt bad about the exchange between Wade and Taylor. She would make it up to Taylor later. Now, all she could think of was being with Wade.

He captured her hand in his, and they walked in the starlight slowly back to the boarding house. Somehow, all the things she wanted to ask seemed unimportant. Her heart was bubbling with happiness. Fool that she was, it seemed all that mattered.

"I have a present for you." Wade said, tucking her hand through his arms tight to his side, "but it isn't wrapped. I'll give it to you in the morning."

You're my present, Mindy thought, but didn't say it.

"We'll spend the day together," Wade announced as though sure she would have no plans of her own. Even if she had, Mindy knew she would have broken them.

At the door, Wade pulled a piece of mistletoe out of his jacket pocket. "I snitched this out of the decorations," he chuckled. He leaned down and tucked it into her hair. Then he put his hand on her cheek, tilted her face up, and kissed her.

"Merry Christmas, little lady."

Somewhere in her dazzled mind, Mindy told herself the Christmas she had almost dreaded had turned out to be the happiest of her life. In her room, Mindy sat in front of her dressing table and removed the mistletoe from her hair. She looked at it for a minute, then realized it was artificial. Of course, where could live mistletoe be found in Coarse Gold? Her next thought chilled her a little: were Wade's words and his kisses also make-believe?

Chapter 18

*O*n Christmas morning, Mindy woke early and went to the special nativity service. Since Wade had made such a point of spending the day together, she wanted to be free to do whatever he had planned without foregoing her customary practice of church attendance.

She did not expect Wade to be at church. To her surprise, however, Taylor was.

She still felt uncomfortable about the way Wade had treated Taylor and determined to put things right with him after the service. Following the closing hymn, the congregation gathered outside to exchange Christmas greetings. Mindy waved and called to Taylor.

At first he seemed reluctant, but when she took a few steps toward him, he came quickly over to her.

"Merry Christmas, Taylor. Wasn't it a lovely service?" He nodded but did not offer anything else. There was nothing to do but to plunge right in to the embarrassing incident at the party. "Taylor, I really apologize about last night."

Taylor looked away, directing his gaze over Mindy's head as though scouting to see if his nemesis was anywhere nearby. Mindy rushed on, "I didn't forget about our dances, it's just that Wade is an old friend, and we hadn't seen each other in a while and—"

"I didn't know you had any *old* friends in Coarse Gold," Taylor interrupted. "You only been here a few months."

Mindy was taken aback. Taylor was sharper than she had given him credit for.

"That's true. What I meant was he's been gone and seeing him so unexpectedly . . . well, I was surprised and—"

"No need to explain, Miss Mindy," Taylor said, twisting his hat in both hands.

"But I didn't want you to misunderstand."

"I don't."

"Well, then, just to be sure I—"

At that moment, Dr. MacAvey hailed Taylor and ambled up to join them. Immediately the subject was changed.

Anxious that Wade might already be at Mrs. Busby's waiting for her, Mindy wished them both a Merry Christmas, excused herself, and hurried back to the boarding house.

To her disappointment he wasn't there. Hours passed, and he still didn't come. Where was he? He had said they would spend the day together. It was not until late Christmas afternoon after she had been watching for him for hours from her bedroom window, that he finally appeared.

He made no apology for tardiness. "Your Christmas present," he said handing her a small carved rosewood box. The coolness with which Mindy had intended to treat him vanished when she opened it. Inside wrapped in satin cloth was a beautiful necklace. On a twisted gold chain hung a heart pendant centered with a brilliant ruby surrounded by tiny diamonds. He gave it to her with deliberate casualness as if to take away any special significance for such an obviously expensive gift.

According to Mindy's traditional upbringing, a lady never accepted jewelry unless engaged to the giver. Such a gift would represent the serious intentions of the gentleman. In her heart, she knew Wade had no such intentions. Still, she wanted to keep it, whatever the motive or its meaning.

For the next few days, Mindy tried to ignore her doubts about Wade. He was charm itself, and she did not want to break the magic spell he cast in which she basked.

She longed for Wade to express his feelings. Until he did she could not declare her own. There was every indication that he enjoyed her company and thought her interesting and attractive. Secretly, Mindy hoped for more.

On New Year's Eve, they joined the party at Mrs. Busby's, agreeing it would be less boisterous than any of the ones taking place at the Palace or at the various saloons in town. In order to offset the number of toasts lifted to the close of one year and the beginning of another, Mrs. Busby had provided a bountiful midnight supper. But in spite of her effort to ring the New Year in with a modicum of decorum, the crowd seemed bent on welcoming the start of a new decade with their own brand of celebration.

Wade and Mindy were surrounded by uninhibited merry-makers. Around them noise swirled, loud voices calling good wishes nearly drowned the music that the band kept valiantly playing. Some celebrants tried to dance. But as the crowd grew every few minutes with people spilling out from the other places on Main Street, to Mrs. Busby's, it was almost impossible. When midnight finally struck, Wade shouted over the tooting of whistles and blowing of paper horns, "Let's get out of here so I can wish you a proper Happy New Year."

He took Mindy by the arm and they made their way through the press of bodies toward the front door and out into the street. The change from the overheated house to the January night was sudden, and Mindy shivered. Wade immediately wrapped her in his arms and, heedless of people passing by, kissed her. A chorus of cheers went up among the onlookers, which brought Mindy back to the reality with a jolt. Quickly she pulled back.

"Wade!" she admonished, conscious that they were surrounded by a circle of laughing bystanders, all of whom began to applaud.

She glanced around embarrassed and stepped away from him, but Wade caught her arm and swung her back. He put one arm around her waist, laughing, "Just wishing you a Happy New Year, Miss McClaren."

But Mindy didn't appreciate being kissed in front of a bunch of leering spectators. She gave him a scathing look and turned on her heel and started walking away. Her intention was to leave him standing there alone. Then she suddenly remembered she lived at Mrs. Busby's. So where could she go to show her disapproval? She stopped short. Wade was right behind her.

"Ah, come on. If I don't care if the whole world sees me kissing you, why should you?" He was amused at her discomfort.

"I just don't like being made a spectacle of on the street."

"Don't worry. They've all had too much to drink. In the morning they'll not even remember what they saw. That is, unless you print it in banner headlines in the *Gazette.*" He seemed to think this hilarious and laughed.

"I don't think that's funny," she said coldly.

Wade raised his eyebrow. "Lost your sense of humor, Miss McClaren?"

Mindy realized she might be making a mountain out of a mole hill. Wade was probably right. In the height of festivity, who would recall or even care the next day?

He came over to her, took her by the hand, and pulled her into the shadows cast by the porch railings of Mrs. Busby's boarding house. There he enclosed her very gently in an embrace and kissed her again. This time it was no ordinary kiss or one given in jest. It had a demanding possessiveness to which she involuntarily responded.

141

She could have drawn away and let him know she had not forgiven him for the impulsive first kiss, but she didn't. She couldn't. Not with the thrill that filled her whole being.

This was a lover's kiss. Wade must really love her..

If she had expected a declaration of love from Wade, Mindy was sadly mistaken. When, two days later Wade left again without telling her what she longed to hear, Mindy was crushed but not shocked. She realized she had to take Wade as he was or not at all. It was up to her to curtail her expectations of the relationship.

For a girl of her pride and independence, Mindy thought, Wade Carrigan held an irresistible fascination. But she could control it she told herself firmly. She had only herself to blame if she let him break her heart.

To mend the ache Wade's going had left, Mindy once again threw herself into her work at the newspaper. She took on more and more of the routine assignments that used to be Byron's. She covered the weekly town council meetings, the court house news, as well as the gatherings of the Women's Temperance Union and the literary society teas. All were dutifully and accurately written up and printed in the *Gazette*.

Mindy was becoming well-known in the community and enjoying a limited respect. The women of the town, who might have looked upon her with some suspicion at first for holding such an unusual job, now regarded her with admiration. Men who might have dismissed her with male superiority now held her in high opinion. Mindy knew much of this was due to Byron's outspoken praise for her as a reporter. She valued and was grateful for that even if that endorsement was verbalized in the watering holes of the town. At least his voice was given attention and Mindy was the recipient of good will.

With Wade gone and evidently out of the way, Taylor renewed his quiet pursuit. He was always polite, almost courtly. From his long residency in Coarse Gold, he knew which social events would occur and would ask to accompany her even before the notice was printed in the *Gazette*. Since Byron usually assigned her to cover such things, Mindy welcomed Taylor's escort. For such a small town, Coarse Gold had an active social schedule. Almost weekly Taylor arrived to take her to church bazaars, performances of the local elocution club, school plays, pie auctions, and other gatherings where the attendance of the town sheriff and the lady editor gave the occasion an added touch.

Taylor was a gentle giant, as many big men are, and had a solid character and high standards of behavior. He was always gentlemanly and never took the slightest liberty. Mindy really was very fond of him, but she did not want to encourage Taylor in any romantic possibilities to their friendship. Perhaps in different circumstances she might have been attracted to the likable lawman. He had all the qualities most women admired: he was honest, kind, responsible. He loved children, as she had seen often, and would be a fine father. But since meeting Wade, no other man could take his place in her foolish heart.

Mindy continued to enjoy her job, even though it sometimes took surprising forms. One day, a grizzly-bearded miner of uncertain age, still dressed in grubby overalls, plaid shirt, worn boots, and battered felt hat, came into the newspaper office. He looked around, then spotted Mindy at her desk and ambled over to her. He doffed his hat and stood for a minute, nervously fingering his soil-stained brim, before he spoke, "Afternoon, miss."

"Can I do something for you?" she asked, wondering what in the world that might be. He held a rolled up newspaper in one hand and rather diffidently held it out to her.

"This here's a Sacramento paper I come by, and in it I seen there's a whole long piece of . . . I dunno 'zactly what you'd call it, but ads." Under his wild beard, his face turned red. "There's quite a few—here see for yerself."

Gingerly, Mindy took the torn-edged paper. It was folded to a section headed PERSONALS. She read the first two on the list.

Struck it rich but lonely. Looking for a woman of sweet disposition to share the rewards with me. Please reply with qualifications to be a congenial companion to well proportioned gentleman, 28 years of age, five-foot-eight of good reputation and health. Will build house to suit lady's taste.

The second was a similar mixture of self praise and humility.

Mindy looked up into the anxious face of the man standing at her desk. As kindly as she could she said, "I'm sorry. We don't carry this type of advertising."

"Yes, ma'am, I knowed that, but I jest thought I might place one of these in that there paper." He twisted his hat and glanced uneasily over his shoulder. He lowered his voice. "You see, I'm sort of like that feller in the first one. My mine done real good—but like the Good Book sez, it ain't good for man to live alone. I been out here a long time, miss, and all the ladies I knew back home has all got married since I left. But I could offer a lot to the right kind of young lady, and I jes' thought this might be a good way to find one."

"How can I help?"

"Well, miss, I ain't much good puttin' words together, and I jest hoped you'd help me word the thing right."

For a minute Mindy started to hand the paper right back to him, but seeing his eager expression, she knew that was impossible. "I can try. Tell me what you want to say, and I'll write it out."

"If we could kinda write it along the lines that fella did, I think that'd do jes' fine."

"Take a seat." Mindy gestured to the chair on the opposite side of her desk. "Now, let's see. We better put your age and a brief description of your appearance." Here she stopped. She heard a choking sound from Byron's desk and looked over to see him struggling not to laugh. She realized he had overheard the whole thing. She threw him a reproving glance, then went back to the man sitting on the edge of his chair, leaning forward. "Your name is?"

"Billy Mahony. And I'm thirty-two. Mebbe you better make that William—sounds more dignified like and mebbe we should say jest past thirty," he suggested.

Mindy suppressed a smile. "Next, physical description. How tall are you, Billy?"

The interview went on without too many hitches. Billy wanted to list all the things he could offer a willing bride. House, furniture of her choosing, a horse and buggy, even one of those newfangled sewing machines.

"This will probably cost you a pretty penny," Mindy cautioned him. "These big California papers charge you by the line or even by the word."

"That don't matter, miss. I got plenty. That's what I want to make clear, I mean, to any young lady who might be reading this."

Mindy wrote on. She read it over a couple of times to Billy, while he nodded and smiled. She made a few substitutions and changes, then copied it down in her neat handwriting and addressed an envelope to the PERSONALS column of the Sacramento newspaper.

"I'm much obliged to you, miss." Billy said, taking it and carefully slipping it into his vest pocket. "Thank you." He took a few steps backward, then, replacing his hat, made his way out of the building.

The door had hardly closed when Byron's amused voice asked, "Going into fiction writing again, are you, McClaren?"

Mindy whirled around and faced him. "What else could I do?"

"Well, nothing I guess. Do you think your reputation as Dixie Dillon has caught up with you?" He laughed. "All that nonsense about Billy's appearance and character. Maybe you better try writing a romance novel."

Mindy was defensive. "I tried to stick to facts. Billy *is* five-feet-ten and does have brown hair, and he said he was going to shave off his beard and just leave the mustache—"

"Then you don't feel guilty giving some poor, unsuspecting woman an idealized picture of the man she might marry?"

"Since you were eavesdropping on the whole thing, you must have heard me say I thought they should carry on a long correspondence before Billy sends her a ticket to come to Coarse Gold."

"And make that a round-trip ticket once she gets a good look at her intended." Byron was getting a good chuckle over this incident. "Oh, well, love is blind as they say. I've seen a lot of people stumble into the wrong relationship because they can't see the forest for the trees."

Mindy tossed her head. "You're full of proverbs, aren't you?"

"Just wisdom gleaned from a long life and experience. I've just seen some very smart ladies make really foolish choices in men."

Mindy glanced at the editor sharply. Was there a not so subtle meaning in what he was saying? And directed at her?

Byron turned back to the copy on his desk saying, "Well, there's no guarantee in any relationship. None whatsoever. Doesn't matter if its a long-distance one or when you see the person every day. You never can know anyone you care about completely."

There was nothing to say to that. Byron's words were true. She realized she didn't know Wade, mainly because he didn't allow her to know him. There was something hidden in him, something guarded. But that was part of his attraction. That mystery behind his eyes, his smile, his easy charm led her on, fed her interest, and made him fascinating.

About this time, a larger room next to Mindy's at the boarding house became vacant and Mrs. Busby offered it to Mindy. "Thought it might be nice for you to have a little sitting room where you could entertain company once in awhile," she said with a little twinkle in her eyes. "Gentlemen callers is fine if you leave the door to the hall ajar, that is."

Mindy gave her a quick look. Nothing much escaped Mrs. Busby. Not only was her dining room the source of local gossip, but she kept an eye on Main Street as well. She probably hadn't missed Wade's comings and goings, nor Sheriff Taylor Bradford's frequent visits, for that matter.

Amused at her landlady's implications she did not supply her with any new information about her social life. "Why, thank you, Mrs. Busby, it would be nice to have a place to put my books, to read, and study more comfortably than down at the office when I have work to do."

Mindy tried not to smile at the look of disappointment on the woman's face, knowing her answer was not what she had in mind when she made the offer.

Mrs. Busby was not easily defeated and quickly retorted, "You do too much of that, my girl. You know what they say about all work and no play . . ."

"I'll remember that," Mindy assured her.

Once acquired, the little parlor did become a place Mindy appreciated, especially the next time Wade rode into town. It also presented a problem she should have anticipated, and it became the scene of a terrible quarrel between them. They had gone to a performance of a play put on by a traveling theatrical troupe. Entertainment in this remote town was rare, and the play was fully attended by most of the community. Coarse Gold boasted no theatre, so the town hall was temporarily transformed into one. The play itself was an appalling melodrama, the actors clumsy and unsure of their lines. Frequent mishaps on stage interrupted the progress of the play. Several loud bangs and crashes from the wings caused the audience to wonder what was happening backstage maybe was more interesting than what was *on* the stage.

For Mindy, the awkward performance did not matter. Although she watched the action and heard the words of the actors, she was too conscious of Wade sitting beside her to notice anything else. If she had been asked to recount the plot or write a review of the play, she would have found it impossible.

During the first two acts she and Wade exchanged glances of amusement at some of the many ludicrous mistakes and stumbling actors. Finally, at intermission, Wade whispered, "I can't take any more. Let's leave."

They slipped out the side entrance and walked back toward Mrs. Busby's. The night air was dry and very cold; snow had lain on the ground since Christmas and their feet crunched on the icy surface. They let themselves in the door of the boarding house. It was unusually quiet because most of the roomers were attending the play. The only person present was the Chinese cook, sleeping in a chair in the pantry way between the kitchen and dining room. They tip-toed past and went into Mindy's newly acquired parlor.

Wade glanced around approvingly, saying with satisfaction. "Now this is more like it." Then striking a theatrical pose he declared dramatically, "Alone at last." He caught both Mindy's hands, twirled her around a couple of times, then pulled her into his arms and began to kiss her.

It had been weeks since they had been together, and at first Mindy returned his kisses ardently. She closed her eyes, surrendering to the tender demand of his mouth on hers. Vaguely recalling Mrs. Busby's forthright admonition that the parlor door be left ajar when Mindy received her "gentleman callers," she slowly opened her eyes and saw Wade had closed the door behind them.

She pushed gently back. "Wade, listen—"

But he wasn't listening. He was kissing her again.

"Wade," she said again, "we can't do this—"

"Why not? Don't be ridiculous, Mindy. The house is empty. No one's here." He held her tighter so she couldn't break away or move. "Let me stay," he said urgently. "No one will be any the wiser."

For the first time in her life, Mindy felt the full impact of temptation. The desire of the moment seemed to wipe out the possibility of regret. Wade drew her closer, kissing her with undisguised intensity. The frightening probability of where this was leading broke into her consciousness. With all her strength, Mindy struggled to free herself and stumbled back from him. She pressed both hands against her mouth, still warm from his kisses. Her breath was shallow, "No, Wade, no."

He looked at her with an expression of disbelief, then disgust. "I thought you were a woman who didn't believe in convention. I believed you were your own person. A daring woman who didn't let others lay down stupid laws of society. Now, I see I was wrong. I guess it was all words, like some of the stuff you write about."

Furious at his indictment Mindy retorted. "This has nothing to do with who I am . . . or maybe, everything to do with who I am."

His mouth twisted. "I said I was wrong, Mindy. About you and what you wanted. At least, I'll take you at your word."

He walked over to the door, yanked it open. "Does this satisfy your puritan soul? I don't play games, Mindy. I play what's on the table. Maybe we're dealing out of two separate decks." His hand turned the knob. "But I'm not sure. I think you wanted me as much as I want you. You just don't have the courage to take a chance that it might be real." He reached for his hat he'd laid on the table when they entered, then made her a slight bow and walked out. Mindy heard his boots on the uncarpeted hallway and a few seconds later the slam of the front door.

She began to shiver. She sank into the nearest chair. She didn't know how long she remained there, frozen, trapped in her tumultuous emotion. Wade had left angrier than she had ever seen him. She had lost him, she was sure of that.

She had seen contempt in his eyes, and his words had stung like a whip on bare flesh. Deepening her anguish was the knowledge that she loved him. But how close she had come to giving in to him and her own desire. She buried her face in her hands, shuddering.

A fragment of Scripture came into her mind, just a few words floating out of context. She went to her bookcase and pulled out the New Testament that she had recently shelved there. It pricked her conscience as she guiltily realized how little of it she had read recently. She thumbed through the pages until memory directed her to 1 Corinthians 10:13, "God is faithful, who will not allow you to be tempted beyond what you are able, but with the temptation will make the way of escape, that you may be able to bear it."

Yes, thank God, and she had applied James 4:7 as well: "Resist the devil and he will flee." God had provided the strength to resist. As badly as her heart was aching, Mindy knew she should be thankful she had avoided worse.

The following day Mindy learned Wade had taken his two horses and left town. Without a good-bye. Why should that surprise her? Why should she have expected one? His bitterly spoken summation of their relationship came back to her. Maybe, they were dealing out of two separate decks. No matter what they felt, neither one would change. She couldn't step over the line that too many years had forged in her of what was morally right or wrong. And for the dozenth time Mindy reminded herself how little she actually knew about him, his background, his beliefs, his life guidelines.

Mindy knew for her own sake she should put Wade Carrigan out of her mind. With discipline that could be done. It wouldn't be so easy to put him out of her heart.

Again, she plunged into her duties at the paper, trying to drown her sorrow with work as Byron tried to drown his with drink. He had fallen off the wagon again, she noticed. But she was too preoccupied with her own heartbreak to try to keep him from making frequent trips to the various saloons. Even during working hours, he would make some excuse and leave, returning visibly unsteady.

Since she had gotten to know Byron, and had learned to recognize the signs that he'd slipped, Mindy had devised a ploy to distract him. She engaged him in conversation, plying him with questions about the business and getting him off on some tangent, like his reminiscences of some sensational story he had covered in the past. But somehow it seemed too great an effort to attempt now. How could she hope to help someone else with a problem when she was having such trouble getting a handle on her own? This was a decision Mindy was soon to regret.

Chapter 19

Startled awake by an incessant banging on her door, Mindy tossed the covers aside and got out of bed, grabbing her dressing gown as she ran barefoot to the door.

A pale, shuddering Timmy, eyes wide with shock, stood in the shadowy hallway. "Oh, miss, come—it's Mr. Karr, and oh, ma'am, I'm afraid he's took bad—"

Mindy knew there was no time to waste. She felt a quivering certainty within that no matter how much she hurried it was already too late. "Wait a minute, until I get on my coat and shoes," she told him. She flung open the wardrobe, pulled out her coat, put it on over her nightgown, slung a shawl over her head and shoulders, and shoved her feet into her boots. She grabbed Timmy's arm as she passed him. "Come on," she said, and they ran down the hall to the front door.

Outside it was bitter cold. "Where is he?" Mindy demanded.

Timmy pointed in the direction of the Golden Slipper and their heads bent against the knife-blade wind as they hurried toward the saloon.

"In there," Timmy panted and dashed past into the narrow passage between the buildings.

Mindy was fast behind him. The sight that met her eyes hit her like a blow. Slumped against the side of the building was Byron's body. She halted, swayed, steadied herself by putting one hand on the wall, then ran to his side. She knelt down on the muddy ground, softened by snow. She put both hands on either side of Byron's face and tried to raise his head. It fell stiffly forward. She slid one hand down his cheek to his neck and felt for a pulse. There was none. She stifled a scream. A cutting wind whistled through the alley, slicing into her, and she shivered. In a hoarse voice she said, "Timmy, run for Dr. MacAvey."

"But, miss, shouldn't we try to move him? Take him home. I done it before when he was like this."

"It's no use, Timmy." Mindy swallowed over the painful lump in her throat. "He's . . . Mr. Karr's dead."

A terrified expression came over the boy's face. Fear filled his eyes. "He can't be. He's jest out. I seen him like this many times. We jest gotta get him to bed—"

"I'm sorry, Timmy. Not this time." Mindy's voice broke. She realized Byron was Timmy's only anchor in his hazardous existence—a father figure for an orphan boy. Without the editor he would have no one. "Now, go. We'll have to have help." She did not want to say the body was already stiffening. She had no idea how long Byron had been dead.

Tears ran down Timmy's freckled cheeks. He swiped his nose with the back of his hand and got up from the crouched position beside her.

"Hurry now," Mindy urged gently.

She watched as the boy started walking back toward Main Street, then break into a run. She turned back to the man she had come to know, respect, and admire in so short a time. What a sad ending for this brilliant man. His eyes were already closed. All she could do was to keep vigil until someone else arrived. She thought of the euphemisms her aunts used when someone died. They never came right out and said someone was dead. They either "passed away" or "crossed over" or, if it was a known relative or church member, "gone to be with Jesus." She didn't really know Byron's spiritual status. Although he quoted broadly from Scripture, she didn't think he attended any church. But kneeling there in the windy corridor between the two saloons, Mindy ardently hoped Byron had "gone to be with Jesus."

It was a raw March day with a wind that cut cruelly as they carried Byron Karr's plain wooden coffin up to the cemetery. Mindy followed, thinking how sad it was this man had died so far from home with neither kith nor kin to mourn him. Mindy knew he had a sister in Pennsylvania, and she remembered vaguely the very courteous nephew she had met the first day she had arrived. But Byron never talked much about himself. If he had ever been married she had no knowledge. Strangely, she felt she knew so many things about him but nothing much about his life before he came to Coarse Gold. That he knew the printing business and had a way with words was obvious. From things he had said inadvertently Mindy knew he had worked at several big-city newspapers back east.

His particular kindness to the "tramp printers" who came occasionally looking for a day's work was a clue that he had some kind of affinity for them. Maybe, sometime, somewhere he too had been down on his luck and in need of a day's pay. Whatever the reason, with the exception of her own father, Byron Karr had been the kindest man she had ever known. Beneath that gruff exterior lay a soft heart. Since his death she had heard countless stories from people he had helped. Miners had come in to tell of "grubstakes" he had replenished for them; a widow left penniless had been given stage fare to get back home. Mindy wished she could print them along with his obituary, which seemed sketchy to say the least, since she knew so little about the editor. Of course, she couldn't. Many of the stories were too private. Byron would hate having his generosity known, much less publicized.

Certainly Mindy had been the recipient of more subtle largesse. He had patiently taught her invaluable things about the newspaper business that only come with long experience. The only thing that worried her was that she may have been too tolerant about his drinking. Could she have done more to prevent his problem instead of looking the other way? She thought of the times on Thursdays, when the paper had been put to bed and she was sitting at her desk, checking her copy, and heard the slide of the bottom desk drawer being opened. That's where he kept his bottle. Could she have done anything? Or does each person have to fight his own demons? She had no idea what Byron was battling to keep at bay.

She looked at the sky. Low clouds hovered. Only a few hardy souls had accompanied the cortege up the hill. It was a week day and most people had to open their shops, attend to their chores, go about the regular business of the living.

Because Byron had not been a church member there was some consternation among those who knew him as to what kind of funeral service there would be. Mr. Proctor, the undertaker, was, of course, right on hand to offer all sorts of suggestions. But Mindy knew Byron would have no interest in one of those. In fact, she recalled his amusement to the ad for the funeral home's "pre-planned programs."

In the end, Mindy decided that she would write a personal farewell to be read at the gravesite, and the minister could add whatever Scripture would be appropriate. She worked long and hard over it, trying to say what was in her heart without being overly sentimental or sorrowful. Byron would have hated flowery language. She could almost hear him say, "Just tell the truth and stick to the facts." So she tried to keep it short, crisp, and yet do proper honor to the man of whom she had become so fond. She had never heard him take the Lord's name in vain, no matter what the provocation, and there were plenty of times at the *Gazette* when one could find an excuse to vent frustrations. She had never heard him pass an unkind remark about anyone, even if one of the advertisers had pulled their ad or someone had given him a tongue lashing over an editorial with which they disagreed. Finally, after several tries, Mindy wrote a single sentence. Now, as she listened to the husky voice of the minister read the words she had chosen for him to read over the grave, she prayed that Byron would be pleased: "Let it be said of him that he reverenced God and loved his fellow man. Well done, good and faithful servant, enter into the rest that is eternal."

Afterward Mindy thanked the minister. She spoke to the others who had also seen Byron to his final repose. Then, along with Timmy, Pete, Dr. MacAvey, and Taylor Bradford, she walked back to town. Mindy's heart felt heavy. She didn't like leaving Byron alone on that windy hill.

When they reached Main Street, Taylor touched Mindy's arm sympathetically. "What are you going to do now?"

"Go to the office."

"I mean . . . now that Karr's gone, will the *Gazette* keep publishing?"

Actually, that was the first time Mindy had had a chance to ask that question herself. She had been too stunned with grief, making arrangements, sending a telegram to Byron's sister, and generally seeing to things. She stared at Taylor.

"This is Tuesday. We've got a paper to get out Thursday." She shrugged. "After that, I don't know."

"I just wondered—I mean, I don't want you to leave Coarse Gold."

Mindy smiled wanly. "I'm not. Not any time soon anyway."

She let herself into the newspaper building. It seemed cold, hollow. Byron had been such a presence there, the hub of the wheel around which everything revolved. Without him there was a huge empty space.

She looked over at his scarred roll-top desk. It had been left open, still cluttered with paper, an open dictionary, and his coffee mug. The tears that had somehow been frozen within her, came now.

Her mind echoed Taylor's question. *What now? How would the paper go on? Would it be for sale? Would someone else come in as editor?* Mindy doubted if Byron had made any provision in case of his death.

Chapter 20

*T*he paper came out on time as usual that Thursday. Mindy had written a glowing eulogy to the late editor, and advertisers had voluntarily come forth with memorial ads for the man who had been more than a friend, "a pillar of the small community"—a phrase many of them used in their space. Mindy felt gratified that in spite of his flaws—failings that had been visible to all—Byron had left a fine legacy, one of which his family could be proud.

It seemed Byron's only immediate family was a sister, Mrs. Rogers, whose name and address Mindy found on letters in Byron's desk. In response to the telegram Mindy had sent informing her of her brother's death, Mrs. Rogers wrote a note addressed to I. Howard McClaren. "Dear Sir," it began,

> Thank you for your kind message concerning my brother Byron Karr's untimely death. He often spoke of his "smart, young assistant editor," and I'm sure you did everything possible to see he had a dignified funeral and Christian burial. As to his personal belongings, *my* thought at the *moment* is to contact my son, who is at present on business in Cali-

fornia. I will suggest he change his plans to travel back to Pennsylvania and come to Coarse Gold instead. I trust he can make the decisions of what I might want of my brother's personal belongings and make disposition of the remainder. Whatever he selects could be packed and shipped here.

Thank you again for your concern and condolences.
Very gratefully,
Mary Alice Rogers

Three weeks went by with nothing settled about the future of the *Gazette,* and no will was located. Mindy was reluctant to go to Byron's cottage and search. The local lawyer declared Byron had never consulted him about making out a will.

In the meantime Mindy, Pete, and Timmy turned out two more editions of the *Gazette.* It was immense pressure and an exhausting strain. Mindy wrote all the articles and helped in the rest of the chores of getting out the paper every week.

Then, three weeks after Byron's death, all of the questions about the fate and future of the *Gazette* were unexpectedly answered. She received a notice to appear at the office of the lawyer Elton Horn for the reading of Byron Karr's will. Elton Horn's office was next door to the undertaker's, which struck Mindy as oddly lugubrious. It was dark and dingy and had an appropriate gloomy air for the kind of professional transactions that must take place within its walls.

The lawyer was a scrawny man, with round shoulders under a dark frock coat. He had a sallow complexion, a short graying beard and deep-set eyes circled darkly as though he got little sleep.

He cleared his throat ponderously after he had ceremoniously bade Mindy to sit down. Then he explained why he had summoned her. It seems that Byron had filed a will in Boulder, and upon the notification of his death, the lawyers who had witnessed the signing contacted Elton Horn, the local lawyer, and sent him a copy.

Mr. Horn said this with an injured air, as though he felt rejected to handle the matter right here in Coarse Gold. Since nothing ever stayed a secret in this small town, Mindy wondered if possibly Byron had taken the precaution not to have the details of his will made common knowledge until after his demise.

Then, with a great show of deliberateness Mr. Horn took out a large portfolio, opened it, and in a voice more like he was about to deliver a court speech than read a will, began. "I, Byron Karr, being of sound mind do declare this to be my last will and testament . . ."

An hour later Mindy walked out of the dim office into the noon sunlight momentarily blinded by the dazzling brightness. She was shocked, surprised, overwhelmed and thrilled. Byron had left the paper and his house to her! The house was for her "to live in, sell or rent as she decided" the will stipulated. These bequests changed everything.

In the past few weeks she had had fleeting thoughts of returning to Woodhaven or even traveling to North Carolina to join her mother and brother. Now all those thoughts disappeared from her mind. She was the owner of the *Roaring River Gazette*. The editor. She had a career, a future, a life here in Coarse Gold. It was something that had not even been in her wildest dreams. But Byron had known it. This was his gift to her.

Mindy walked up on the hillside cemetery. There was only a simple wooden cross to mark the place where they had laid Byron. Only his name was carved on it. No one seemed to know the date or place of his birth. Mindy stood absolutely still as she looked at it, remembering the day she had first met him. He had trusted her, had faith in her, believed in her. By leaving the paper to her he had passed the torch so that the things he valued could go on.

It had all happened so fast the past few weeks, Mindy had not had enough time to absorb the reality of it all. She had dreamed of becoming a reporter and now she was an editor. Yet her belief that everyone has a purpose, that God has a definite plan for each life, suggested to her that this had been the unknown reason she had always felt so restless. Nothing had really satisfied or fulfilled her before. The more she thought about this, Mindy felt a confirmation. This was why she had come to Colorado—not on a whim or a reckless impulse, but because it was her destiny.

Mindy closed her eyes, bent her head into her clasped hands, and prayed the most sincere prayer of her life. A prayer of thanksgiving for who she was and for guidance of how she should use her talents. The influence of the position of editor was daunting, but with God's help Mindy trusted she would use it wisely.

Chapter 21

One afternoon a few weeks later, Mindy was finishing up at her desk when the newspaper office door opened and a man entered. He stood on the threshold for a minute, glancing around as if looking for someone. Mindy raised her head and asked, "Yes? Something I can do for you?"

"I hope so. I'm looking for I. H. McClaren."

Mindy studied him for a moment before answering. He was of average height, neatly dressed in eastern looking clothes. He had removed his hat and with one hand smoothed back thick, wavy, light brown hair. He took a few steps forward coming to stand directly in front of her desk so she had a better view of him. He was young, about thirty, clean-shaven with well-formed features and a pleasant expression. There was something vaguely familiar about him but she could not place him. At the same time he was regarding her with keen interest.

"You don't remember me, do you?" he asked, "I'm Byron's nephew. We met briefly, but it's been a long time ago, over a year."

Mindy remembered her first day in Coarse Gold. Byron had gone to see his nephew off on the train, and she had been introduced to him at the station. Before that there had been a brief encounter at the hotel. He had held the door open for her. "Of course. I'm sorry. It *has* been a long time and so much has happened—" She couldn't help but wonder whether he knew that Byron had left the *Gazette* to her. Had he come to take it over himself? For an awful moment, Mindy thought about how she could explain things if that was his intention. She swallowed and gestured to the chair beside her desk. "Please, sit down. I'm so sorry about your uncle. He was a wonderful man and a good friend."

"Thank you." He took a seat, still regarding her intently and with some curiosity. "My mother's letter just caught up with me. I've been traveling throughout California, and it was only when I got back to my hotel in Sacramento that I found out about Uncle Byron's death."

"Yes, it was very sudden and unexpected," Mindy said, wondering if she should leave out the details.

"At my mother's request I changed my ticket and came here as soon as I concluded my business. She wanted me to go through my uncle's belongings and make some decisions about their disposal. Of course, there may be a few mementos she would like that are of sentimental value. He was her older brother, her only brother, and although they had not seen each other in several years, Mother loved him dearly, in spite of—" He broke off, then said, "My mother did not always approve of—well, they did have some differences as all families do."

"I have the keys to Byron's little house. As you know, he left that to me in his will as well," said Mindy. "I'll give them to you so that you can find whatever you want. You may even be able to make arrangements with the station manager to have them packed and shipped."

"A good idea. Thank you—" He paused, "I'm sorry I don't know your name, I'm afraid."

"McClaren," she supplied. "And yours?"

"I beg your pardon, I should have introduced myself. I'm Lawrence Day." His smile broadened revealing excellent teeth. "Could you possibly be Mindy? Mother just said she had received a letter from I. H. McClaren. She assumed it was a man but—I should have guessed right away. Uncle wrote us so much about 'Mindy.'"

"Are you aware that in his will your uncle left the paper to me?" Mindy thought that perhaps a copy of the will had been sent to Byron's sister, Mr. Day's mother. Again, she wondered whether Byron's nephew might want to contest the will and take over the newspaper. That suspicion made her cautious. He looked perfectly amiable, however, not as though he had come ready to do battle for an inheritance.

"No, I didn't know that—though he wrote me that he had a great new assistant editor. I know he must have felt you were competent."

"Even though it's considered to be an unusual position for a woman to fill?"

He smiled. "Maybe, back east they still feel that way. But I've discovered out west that women hold all sorts of jobs— run businesses, own department stores and restaurants, have many positions and do them well. In some cases, better than men."

Mindy looked at him with surprise. "That's a very enlightened attitude."

"I hope so. The world is changing fast, and out west you see it firsthand. I like to keep up with the times."

"Byron and I worked together for nearly a year before his death. I didn't know he was ill. I saw he was slowing down but thought it was mostly—" She cut her sentence short.

A shadow passed over the nephew's face—regret, compassion? Then he sighed, "It was only a matter of time. I think we all knew that when he came west. You see, my uncle suffered a tragic loss." He paused and lifted his eyebrows. "Perhaps, you didn't know about it. He never looked for sympathy or tried to gain it. He lost his wife and child in a fire and after that ... well, he was never the same. He came out here to forget, to try to build a new life, but—"

"He helped me so much," Mindy said. "He taught me the ropes of running a newspaper. He was a very kind man."

Lawrence Day saw Mindy's blue eyes brighten with tears, and he was struck by this show of emotion. Evidently this young woman cared deeply about his uncle whom he himself hardly knew. He wished he had known him better.

"Yes, he was. I was always very fond of him. My own father died when I was just a little boy and although I had a great stepfather, Uncle Byron was special." He stopped for a minute, "Well, I'm sure you're busy, Miss McClaren, so I'd better get on with my mission. I leave tomorrow on the noon train." He took the keys Mindy handed him and stood up, "I better find myself a place to stay overnight."

"The Palace is about the best you can do, Mr. Day. It's just down the street on the corner."

"It was a pleasure to meet you Miss McClaren. I think my uncle made a wise choice."

"Thank you." Mindy felt her face warm.

He hesitated. "If I wouldn't be out of line suggesting it— would it be possible for us to have dinner together? There is so much I'd like to know, to ask about my uncle. You see I didn't know him very well these last years ... none of us did ... not my mother nor my stepfather. You, of all people, might have the answers to some of my questions."

Mindy debated only a few seconds. "Why, yes, thank you. I would be happy to have dinner and answer any questions I could."

"Splendid. Is the hotel all right? I mean for dinner."

"Well, actually, Mrs. Busby's is better. Better food and not so crowded. She'd give us a table to ourselves where we could talk quietly. The Palace tends to get pretty noisy, especially on Fridays when the miners and cowboys come into town for the weekend."

He held out his hand. "Good enough. Mrs. Busby's it is then. We'll meet there at six, right?" He smiled, and that was when Mindy realized what had seemed familiar about him. He had the same smile as Byron.

Lawrence Day left the newspaper office and walked down the street with a sure step. He was impressed. He really hadn't known what to expect of his uncle's assistant editor. He had liked the feel of her small hand in his when she had shaken it. In spite of her direct manner and obvious ability, there was something gentle and womanly about her. She hardly reached his chin, but she held herself erect and those eyes—he had never seen such eyes. Their color reminded him of what? Gentians in the fall or the first berries of summer? Bright and a deep blue. Suddenly the arduous trip he had made by train and stage from California that he'd undertaken as a family duty had taken a different tack. He found himself looking forward to having dinner with Miss Mindy McClaren.

Mrs. Busby was happy to meet Byron's nephew. She had always had a soft spot for the editor, even sending him meals over on a tray when he was recovering from one of his lost weekends.

As she seated them at a window table, she asked, "What will you folks have tonight? Chicken and dumplings is the choice for tonight. 'Course we always have steak for them that wants it. Hash browns with onions."

Knowing that chicken and dumplings were Mrs. Busby's specialty, Mindy chose that and Mr. Day followed suit.

While they were waiting for their order he told Mindy he was a manufacturer's representative for a line of tools. Because of the rapid development in the west he was sent by his company to place their products with hardware stores and builders. "You'd be surprised how much interest there is in the west back east. For awhile, during the war, it was almost forgotten. And the west seems hardly to have been touched by what was happening there. It's been really an eye-opener to me. People here are eager to have the latest tools, the newest—so my trip has been quite successful."

Their dinner came, and while they ate they found so much to talk about they hardly noticed that their dessert of deep dish apple pie was served, and their coffee mugs were refilled three times. Suddenly, Mindy looked around and exclaimed. "Good heavens, it must be late." The dining room had emptied and they were the only two left.

"The time has certainly passed quickly and so pleasantly I hadn't noticed. I haven't kept you from anything you had planned, I hope?" Day looked anxious. "No, not at all. But I do have to go in early tomorrow. Thursday, you know." She started to get up, and Day came around to draw back her chair. Mindy smiled, Byron's nephew had the gentlemanly manners sadly lacking out here, ones she had almost forgotten still existed.

Mindy asked, "Did things go well at Byron's house?"

"There were such a great many books that I thought it would be useless to try to go through them in such a short time as I have. I packed a few things, some photographs, for instance, and some other things my mother would like to have. I think I may come back here on my next business trip and plan to spend a few days, or even a week, to do a complete inventory and make definite deposition." He paused. "In the meantime, Miss McClaren, why don't you take advantage of Byron's fine library? He has all the classics and other books I'm sure you'd find interesting. I know he would like that."

"That is most kind of you. I may well take you up on your offer."

They stopped on the way out of the dining room, and he complimented Mrs. Busby on the meal. "It was the best meal I've had since coming west." She beamed.

He walked with Mindy to the door of her little parlor. He held out his hand, smiling. "Sometimes, in his letters, my uncle exaggerated—the writer in him, I suppose. However, he did not exaggerate in your case. Good night, Miss McClaren, thank you for your help. It's been a real pleasure."

"For me, too, Mr. Day. I hope you have a good trip home. Let me know if and when you plan to be back in Coarse Gold."

"That I will surely do, I promise."

As she undressed and got ready for bed, Mindy thought over the evening. It *had* been pleasant—one of the pleasantest she had spent in a long time. She had missed conversation with an intelligent, interesting person. It reminded her of some of the talks she and Byron had had together, and she missed the editor all over again. His nephew was very like him. Too bad he was leaving town. It might be nice to get to know him better. Maybe, if he did return to Coarse Gold . . . but then you never know. People said things, made plans but sometimes they didn't work out.

PART 3

PART 3

Chapter 22

*A*fter her first excitement, Mindy realized that taking over the editorship of the *Gazette* was far more difficult than she had ever imagined. She worked all hours. She came in some mornings just as it was getting light and stayed late, working by the flickering oil lamp at her desk. It seemed she had no other life but running the newspaper. Now, she had to do everything: sign up advertisers, layout copy, write articles and editorials, oversee the finished copy, help run the press, see the pages inserted and the paper folded, ready to deliver. She kept saying the paper needed more help. But where could she get it? Who could she find to take some of the more menial jobs that never seemed to get done? Coarse Gold was a miners' town. That's where the money was, and everyone was trying to find it up in the hills.

Although Mindy took great pride in what she was accomplishing almost single-handedly, it was taking its toll. By Thursday evening she was so tired she practically swayed on her feet with fatigue. Often, it was all she could do to put one foot in front of the other to make her way down the street back to her room. There she would fall, utterly exhausted, onto her bed.

She kept telling herself it was worth it. Dreams didn't come cheap. By Monday she was ready to start the next week's grinding pace again. The real reward was that she had proved something to herself—and to those who thought Byron had made a mistake, trusting a woman to run a newspaper.

The price she was paying, however, narrowed her life considerably. She didn't have time now to stop and chat with people if she was out to get a story, which was almost always. She didn't have time to nurture friendships that would have been helpful to her, nor to make new friends. Life was distilled to work.

About two months after Byron's death, late one afternoon, Mindy was working at her desk when she had heard unusually loud noises from outside. She cocked her head, then went back to work, too busy to pay much attention. The noise suddenly swelled frighteningly. It sounded like the roar of a train hurtling down the track head-on. Mindy frowned and got to her feet. The shouting was too loud to ignore. She left her desk and went through the newsroom, out to the front porch. She saw people running, rushing down the street toward the sheriff's office and jail. She went down a couple of steps, grabbing the arm of a young boy passing by. "What's going on?"

"A hangin'," he yelled, tugging his sleeve from her grasp.

"But the sheriff's out of town." She said. She knew because Taylor had come by to tell her good-bye the other day, reminding her wistfully that they hadn't had any time together in weeks. "Sheriff Bradford's gone—," she repeated, but the boy paid no attention. He pulled away and kept running.

Mindy's heart began to pump heavily. A hanging? She didn't know of any trial that had taken place in the last week or any sentences for a hanging. Taylor had come by before leaving to pick up a prisoner to be tried for cattle rustling under Judge Moltry's jurisdiction. The ranch from which they were stolen was on the outskirts of Coarse Gold. So who could have given a verdict to hang someone—and for what crime?

Mindy ran down the rest of the steps and found herself in the middle of the throng, pushed and shoved along the street by the crowd, moving like a mighty tide to the jailhouse. Already a large group had gathered there. She tried to elbow her way to the front, but the bodies were too tightly packed for her to get through. Her hairpins had fallen out and her hair was trailing down her neck. She gathered it with both hands and pushed it back. She tried standing on tip-toe so she could see over the heads and shoulders of people blocking her view.

The din around her was deafening. She jerked the sleeve of a man standing next to her and raised her voice to be heard over the crowd. "Who is it?"

He turned and looked down at her. "A drifter. Caught redhanded trying to get away with a horse from the livery stable. But they nabbed him. He's gonna git what's comin' to him. Seems folks know him from way back. He's a no-good."

"But Sheriff Bradford's out of town," Mindy protested. "They can't hang a man without a hearing." But her informant wasn't listening. He had joined in the jeering and yelling that was rising like a flood.

Fierce indignation welled up in Mindy. They couldn't do this. They couldn't take the law into their own hands. This was primitive, uncivilized behavior. It belonged to the past, to vigilante days, not the enlightened present—Not now when there was law. This was criminal.

The noise all around her rose as in one dreadful shout. The roar of the crowd drowned out any protests, if there were any other than her own. Then a terrible hush fell.

Voices died down into a rumble. Then a kind of hoarse echo of muttering as people in front began to break away, leaving, scattering in small groups.

Little by little the crowd thinned, but Mindy remained standing there as if rooted to the ground. Now that she could see straight ahead, she saw a dangling body swinging against the darkening sky. Her stomach lurched and she turned away.

Shocked and miserable, she staggered back to the newspaper office. At the steps she felt a wave of nausea sweep over her. She stumbled to the side of the building and was sick.

She never knew how long she sat alone in the newsroom at her desk, shaking with impotent rage at what had happened in the town she had come to love. That people would be capable of such malicious lawlessness in this peaceful community stunned her. She felt helpless and hopeless, paralyzed by what she had observed. The image of the hanged man would be etched forever on her mind.

Slowly she drew a piece of paper in front of her, dipped her pen in the inkwell, and began to write with a passionate fury. "YOU CALL YOURSELVES MEN?" She wrote. Then she underlined it, marking for Pete that the headline should be set in bold type. Thursday's edition would bear evidence of her shame, guilt, and indictment of the town for the obscene act she had witnessed.

On Friday the newspaper office was empty. Pete and Tim had long since gone. Mindy was alone. She had not felt like going back to her room. There, the loneliness would seem even greater.

At six it was already dark. The single light from the oil lamp on Mindy's desk illuminated her reflection in the opaque rectangle of the front window facing the street.

Mindy knew she had to rid herself somehow of the creeping depression. She longed to get back her old enthusiasm for her work. She did not like the feeling of alienation she now saw among the people she had worked so hard to make friends. Suspicion, resentment, and worse—hostility and anger. It hadn't been easy getting them to accept her even when Byron was alive. It had been even more difficult for them to respect her as an editor. But now, why was she being vilified for standing up for decency? For exercising Christian values?

In the months since Byron's death she had felt more confident all the time. Now she wondered if she had assumed too much by taking her bold stands and separating herself from the prevailing sentiment of the community of which she wanted to be a part.

Her editorial had been fiery. Written in the heat of her disgust and outrage, she had not tested its content with anyone. Even Pete had raised his eyebrows a little when she gave it to him to set. But justice was justice. Taking the law into their own hands was wrong. Yet lines had been drawn about her speaking out against them.

Now self-doubt plagued her. Had she acted too hastily, too impulsively? No, unconsciously Mindy banged her small fist on the desktop. She knew she was right. She had confronted all of them, even those who had just stood by silently while a man was hung without a trial. She had demanded they search their consciences. Compassion for another human being was what she had demanded of them. Fairness, that's all.

Even Taylor, when he returned, was reticent. As a lawman, of course, he deplored the hanging. But he didn't wholeheartedly support her taking on the whole town. It was the first time anything had come between them to disturb the pleasant companionship they shared and the possibility, at least in Taylor's mind, that it might develop into something deeper. He didn't tell her, but she knew even the people who weren't happy about what had taken place in his absence had complained about the editorial. She could imagine the whispers: "Who does she think she is?" "A woman don't have no business being a newspaper editor."

If she had been a man, would it have been the same? Mindy didn't think so. While some might consider her brave—a fearless crusader for any man's right to a trial, no matter what his past—Mindy knew there were others who felt just as strongly opposite, calling her a meddling woman poking her nose where didn't belong. After all, everyone said Janus McCabe was a known rustler and horse thief.

All at once Mindy felt a tingling along her scalp. Her whole body seemed to quiver to alertness, brace. Then she heard the crash and the shattering of glass as a rock was hurled through the front window, sending splinters flying everywhere.

The next day she still felt shaky, in spite of Taylor's adamant assurance he would catch the culprit. Taylor had arrived at the newspaper office within minutes after the window was shattered. People in the street had heard it and ran to get him at Mrs. Busby's. He still had his napkin tucked into his belt as he had rushed over from the dining room where he had been eating supper. He had his hand on his holster ready to draw his gun as he rushed into the newspaper office, demanding, "You all right, Mindy?"

She was leaning against her desk, her knees weak and wobbly, unable to speak. He came over to where she was and put a hand awkwardly on her shoulder.

"Yes, I'm all right." She nodded and tried to take a deep breath.

He stood patting her comfortingly while looking around the newsroom. "Wait a minute," he said and took a few steps over to the window, his boots crunching on the broken shards on the floor. Then he bent down and picked up a sizeable rock. A piece of paper was tied to it wrapped with a frayed string of twine. He examined it, then told Mindy,

"Something's printed on it. Can't make it out," but his face was flushed an angry red.

Mindy held out her hand for it. "Here let me see it, maybe I can."

Taylor shook his head, his mouth folded grimly. "No Mindy. From what I can see, it ain't fittin' for a lady to read."

"Don't be silly, Taylor. If it's about me I want to see it. Maybe we can tell who did this."

Taylor shook his head again. "This is sheriff's property, evidence. You have to be a deputy to view evidence at the scene of a crime."

Even though frustrated, Mindy had to suppress a smile. Although it might be Lawman Bradford asserting his authority, she knew actually it was something else. Taylor's inherent gentility prevented him showing Mindy the derogatory note—even though she was the newspaper's editor and this was quite a story. As far as Taylor was concerned, Mindy was first a lady, to be protected.

In spite of her show of calm, the incident had shaken Mindy badly. For the next few days, she started at the slightest sound and had to curb her tendency to look over her shoulder when she went in or out of the newspaper office. She was especially nervous if required to stay late for some reason. It didn't matter that she told herself not to be afraid, that nobody would dare really harm her. She had lost some of her innocence and knew she would never get it back. Had it been worth speaking her mind so forcibly in the editorial? Just as she had felt in the disastrous aftermath of her Dixie Dillon exposé of the housemaids living conditions in Woodhaven, she was still glad she'd done it. If they ran her out of town . . . well, maybe that was the price she had to pay.

For all the cold looks and the obvious shunning by people who turned away at her approach, Mindy was determined to confront the coward who had thrown the rock and smashed the newspaper window. Reminding herself of

Byron's oft repeated remark, "The pen is mightier than the sword," Mindy sat down to use the weapon she knew best.

Scripture was always a powerful way to attack wrongdoers, so she indicated a headline for her retaliatory editorial: "HE WHO IS WITHOUT SIN CAST THE FIRST STONE," she wrote with the same fluidity of the first one.

> If my sin is calling an action a sin and a spade a spade, then I'm guilty. In my opinion, that is an editor's duty. To bring to the attention of a community something corrosive in its midst that, if unchecked, unhealed, will eventually destroy our town. We are progressive, right-thinking people. We employ the Golden Rule. We believe in the basic principles for which our country stands: Liberty, Justice, Equality. Every man is entitled to a trial. That is the law of our land. When rabble-rousers overstep this right, they are committing a crime—a sin if you will—and endangering their own lives should fate ever bring them into a similar situation. Circumstantial evidence is not enough. The Bible requires the testimony of at least two witnesses. Why didn't anyone speak up for the poor wretch that lawbreakers hung? Was there no one brave enough to do so? Whoever he was, he was a human being like the rest of us. Unknown to us he had a mother who will weep and mourn for him. Perhaps a wife and children. We will never know. We did not give him a chance. And this town will carry the burden of guilt and shame for this lawless act. Because I live here and work here and have come to know and consider many of you my friends, I beg you to pledge with me that never again will such a shameful act be done in the name of so-called justice.

When Pete read it before setting it in type, he gave Mindy a wry grin. "That's tellin' 'em," he drawled. Mindy felt gratified, because Pete was a miser with compliments.

The next week after the paper came out and was circulated, Mindy was conscious of some approving nods and some tentative smiles as she walked down the street. A bunch of early wildflowers appeared on her desk when she came back from lunch, and several commending letters to the editor trickled in over the next few days.

Mindy had the definite feeling that the town had taken a good hard look at itself, given itself a shake, squared its shoulders, and faced the future with a renewed determination to make itself proud again. More than that, she felt she had gained some new respect, if not agreement—at least that she was a force to be reckoned with.

The following week, Mindy was just cleaning up some copy one afternoon when she heard a deep, familiar voice , "Good day to you, Miss McClaren."

Her head jerked up and she half rose from her desk, "Wade!" Then not wanting to seem too glad to see him, she sat back down and tried to assume a casual air. How dare he saunter in so nonchalantly as if nothing had happened between them at New Year's? Well, she could be just as cool as he. "What brings you back in town?" She shuffled some papers as if busy and not particularly interested in his answer. But the edginess in her voice showed her irritation.

"Oh, this and that," he said casually. "Heard you had a mite of trouble since I've been gone. Was anyone hurt?"

"No, I was here by myself and no one was hurt."

He swore softly under his breath. "Why'd you take that kind of risk? There are a lot of hotheads around here; once they get boozed up, they're just looking to pick a fight."

"Against a defenseless woman?" she scoffed. "Takes some kind of man to do that!"

"Maybe the same kind of man who strings somebody up without the law."

Mindy raised her eyebrows and shrugged, but did not comment.

179

Wade came closer, put both hands on her desk and leaned forward. "Well, you must admit you took a chance."

"Of telling the truth?"

"I just don't see it as a woman's place to tell men what they should or should not do."

"I didn't realize decency and justice belonged exclusively to men. Women are just as affected by vigilantism and injustice as men. And they have just as much right to speak out against wrong-doing when they see it."

Wade stepped back, held up both hands as if to protect himself. "Well, if you aren't a spitfire-of-an-editor for sure."

Mindy flung down her pencil and stood up.

"Don't patronize me, Wade."

He gave a soft, low laugh. "Patronize? I wouldn't do that, Mindy. I think you're adorable . . . especially when you're defending your rights."

"You're doing it now. Thinking you can soften me up with all these compliments. I know what you really like in a woman—someone compliant, soft-spoken, submissive—"

"Just a minute, young lady. What I was going to say, that is if you'd give me half a chance—" He came around to her side of the desk, "—is that while your methods may be admirable, your indignation justified, I just question your telling off the men of this town the way you did." He put his hand on her arm. " To quote my dear old grandmother, 'You can catch more flies with honey than vinegar.'"

Mindy shook off his hand, "Well, far be it from me to contradict your grandmother."

Wade laughed. "You *are* adorable when your dander's up." He pulled her close, wrapped his arms tightly around her so she couldn't move. Finding her struggle futile, she relaxed, leaned against his chest, her heart thumping. With one hand he smoothed back her hair. Then, with the other hand on the back of her neck, he tipped her chin up so she had to look at him and in a low coaxing voice asked, "Did you miss me?"

All her anger melted away. She *had* missed him. More than she wanted to admit to herself. More than she would ever tell him.

Chapter 23

*W*ith Wade's return Mindy was determined not to be swept away again. She knew how dangerously close she had come to flinging away everything she valued. She recognized Wade was her temptation, and she was determined to resist him, unless his own attitude changed. Which was possible. Mindy noticed that since he'd come back there was *something* different about him.

He seemed more thoughtful, less sarcastic, gentler. She dared to hope that, perhaps, he might even want more than a temporary fling. He seemed to have a new respect for her work, which she found heartening. Though he remained an enigma, their companionship had subtly changed. She didn't allow her imagination to take flight, but tried to enjoy the moment, the time they spent together, without dreaming of the future.

One thing Mindy had missed since coming to Coarse Gold was having a woman friend. In Coarse Gold, she was unique. Even the schoolteacher was male. She longed for someone in whom she could confide, could share her intimate feminine feelings. Most of the women in the community had followed their miner husbands here and were fully occupied with making a home for them and having babies. There was no one who could understand the stress and worries and problems Mindy knew as a single, working woman.

That is why she was elated the day Elyse Sinclair arrived in town. That day, as the stage from Sacramento pulled in, Mindy was just coming out of the general store after securing the ad for next week's edition. Like everyone else in town the arrival of the stage was always the highlight of the day. Curious folks always gathered to see who got off and to guess their reason for coming.

When Mindy saw a tall, thin woman get off, she paused. The first thing she noticed about her was her traveling outfit. She wore a belted tan jacket of serviceable cotton over a skirt that barely reached the ankles of sturdy boots. A soft-brimmed felt hat shadowed her face so that Mindy couldn't determine her age or see her expression. Mindy watched the woman engage the stage driver in directions for lowering her belongings from where they were lashed on top. These turned out to be a tripod and two large, bulky leather bags. Then the woman turned and pulled out another heavy leather bag approximately the same size from the interior.

As she slung it by its wide strap over her shoulder, she caught Mindy staring at her and immediately smiled and waved, "Hello there."

Such open friendliness was a surprise. Mindy crossed over preparing to introduce herself. The other woman extended her hand and gave Mindy's a firm shake. "I'm Elyse Sinclair." Her eyes were as clear and candid as a child's, and her smile revealed a beautiful set of teeth. She pulled a small card out of her pocket and handed it to Mindy. "E. SINCLAIR, PHOTOGRAPHER: Artistic Pictures to Cherish of Loved Ones, Children, Groups. All Occasions. Weddings, a Specialty."

"Welcome to Coarse Gold. I'm Mindy McClaren, editor of the *Roaring River Gazette*."

"A lady newspaper editor? That's almost as rare as a woman photographer—"

Mindy looked at several more boxes and bags being piled around Elyse by the stagehand. Elyse followed the direction of Mindy's gaze.

"Yes, it takes a great deal of equipment. That's why I have to find a place big enough to store all this and, if I'm lucky, a place to develop my negatives." She paused. "As the editor of the town newspaper, you must have a wealth of information. Could you suggest where I could find rooms to rent and some place I could work?"

Mindy thought for a minute. Byron's house had been left to her along with the paper. After Lawrence Day had packed the editor's personal belongings he thought his mother might want, Mindy had simply closed the place up. She hadn't received any further instructions of what to do with the rest of the contents of the cottage. Maybe, Elyse Sinclair would want to rent it? With just a moment's hesitation, Mindy suggested this.

Elyse was enthusiastic. "That sounds perfect. Could you show it to me? That way I can haul my stuff right over there instead of having to move it twice."

As they walked the short distance to Byron's cottage, Elyse told Mindy she had a commission from a Geographic Society interested in photographs of the west. "They want a picture story of how the towns—once just a conglomeration of slapped-together mining shacks—are now developing, how communities are forming, what the people and life out here are like now." She gave Mindy an appraising glance. "From the look of things, it is farther advanced than most of the small towns back east. If you don't mind my asking, how are you accepted—I mean, as a woman running a newspaper?"

"Depends on who you ask, I guess," Mindy laughed.

They reached Byron's small house, and Mindy took out a ring of keys, found the right one, and unlocked the door.

Elyse was thrilled with the neat little house and wanted to take it immediately. Mindy had not even thought how much rent she should ask, but that did not seem to matter to Elyse.

"This is marvelous," Elyse exclaimed as she walked through. "Could I use one of the rooms as a dark room?" She darted an anxious look at Mindy, "There'd be chemicals and developing fluids. Smell awful but relatively harmless if you know what you're doing."

"Well," Mindy said slowly. "I have a better idea. There's a shed behind the newspaper building you could use for that. That way you wouldn't have to breathe the stuff when you're here."

"Wonderful," Elyse clapped her hands. "You're a genius, Miss McClaren." She put her head to one side and gave Mindy a speculative look. "It is miss isn't it?"

Mindy blushed, thinking of her former fantasies about Wade, but answered, "Yes, it is miss, but please call me Mindy."

Elyse's smile lighted her eyes, which made her plain face almost attractive. "Good. I think we're going to be great friends, Mindy."

That happened sooner than Mindy could have imagined. After the first meeting, they found each other congenial companions. Within a short time, they recognized similar traits in each other that naturally drew them closer.

Until Elyse came, Mindy hadn't fully realized just how lonely she was or how much she had missed having a woman to talk to. Elyse was six years older than Mindy and had already made several important decisions about her life, including the decision never to marry and have children. This came out one evening when they were sharing their supper.

"I don't see any way to do that and be true to myself. Once I discovered photography, I knew it was going to be my life's work. It is so absorbing, requires so much concentration, so much dedication to really succeed, it wouldn't be fair to a man to give him half a wife. Marriage, I believe, is something that takes your whole devotion. And children—well, they would be neglected if they had a mother whose main interest was elsewhere."

"Was that a difficult decision?" Mindy asked, thinking it could be a decision she might one day have to make. Had Elyse ever had a romantic attraction to someone? Had she given it up to pursue her career? At Mindy's question something passed over Elyse's face momentarily, leaving it pensive. Regret? Sadness? Memories of a relinquished romance?

"Only difficult insofar as you never quite know if it *was* the right decision, not knowing what you might be missing, what you might have been able to handle given the right man, the right situation ... but ... no, in the end, it was pretty easy. And I'm a great believer in living in the present, not looking back."

Their friendship developed rapidly, and their times together fell into a pleasant routine. After both had finished their day's work, they would meet either in Mindy's parlor or at Byron's old cottage. There they would share the events of the day or make plans. More often than not, their conversations took a decidedly philosophical turn. Marriage was a subject that seemed to hold special interest for discussion. At least for Mindy.

One day, as the fire in the little potbelly stove crackled, Elyse smiled ruefully. "I'm not a gambler," she said, "and marriage seems to me the biggest game of chance imaginable." She took a sip from her mug of cocoa. "My sister, for instance. I can still see her on her wedding day, stars in her eyes, happiness radiating from her expression." Elyse shook her head and bit her lower lip as if thinking of something with great sadness.

Mindy was curious to hear the rest of the story. "What happened? Wasn't she happy?"

"Happy? Ten years later, with seven children, I'm not sure. How can anyone on the outside really know about a marriage but the two people involved." She paused. "I'm just saying what I've observed. If she isn't happy, it's not Steven's fault. He's a good man, good provider, good father, I'm sure. It's simply that too many people go into marriage believing that a person is going to fulfill all their expectations, make all their dreams come true. But that's too heavy a burden for anyone to bear."

"What should marriage be then?"

Elyse took another sip of cocoa before replying. "I don't know if it can be anything different than what it is now. But I should think the only way two people can live together happily is with respect for who the other person is. Who they *really* are, not who they think they should be."

Mindy was quiet. She thought of all the ways she wished Wade would change. Was that too much to expect? Could she live with someone she felt she didn't understand, someone who never explained himself. Wade liked complete freedom, to come and go and do whatever he wanted with no questions asked. That was no basis for a lasting, loving relationship much less a marriage.

Suddenly, Mindy felt the need to confide her ambivalence about Wade. The other young woman looked interested but cautious.

"Never having met the gentleman, it'd be hard for me to give you advice. I just know from my own experience that it's a rare man who can share his wife with her work. I don't know why. Women certainly are able to support a man's, whatever it is, and follow him wherever he goes, make a home in whatever barren land that happens to take him. I know. I've seen it. I've photographed it!"

Mindy took a long breath and confessed, "We've never talked about the future, Wade and I. When I'm with him everything seems to be—I don't know—so special, so exciting that I don't think of anything else." She paused. "But then he's . . . well, sort of mysterious. He comes and goes. He doesn't like to be asked questions or say where or when . . ." She winced, then made a comic face. "And you can imagine what that does to a newspaper reporter! He always tells me to stop interviewing him."

"He sounds like someone with a dark past." Elyse raised her eyebrows.

"Oh, everyone out here has some kind of past—something they're trying to forget, or is too painful to remember. Coarse Gold is full of men who've burned their bridges behind them."

Mindy remembered Byron Karr. And she hadn't learned much more about him from his nephew either.

"What about the handsome lawman I see hovering around you everywhere? Now he's my idea of a real hero straight out of *True West* magazine," Elyse teased. "He's obviously head over heels in love with you."

"Oh, Taylor," Mindy dismissed the suggestion. "Taylor is the proverbial open book. Plain and solid."

"So it's mystery and the unknown that fascinates you." Elyse lifted her eyebrows again. "Then my advice is that you better stay single."

Elyse's comment hit close to the mark. Mindy knew that it was Wade's mysterious aura that intrigued her. She was mindful of the problems in "loving not wisely but too well." Was that the narrow precipice she was walking with Wade? Were her feelings teetering close to the edge, where any minute she could plunge into the depths?

She had tried to tell herself Wade Carrigan was too vain, too self-absorbed, too indulgent of his own pleasures to ever commit himself. Physical attraction was one thing, but love? Was he capable of true, enduring love of the kind Mindy wanted?

As little as he told her about himself, sometimes Mindy thought she saw a look of melancholy in his eyes, as if there were unrealized dreams, unfulfilled promise or regrets. She found it hard to think about a future with Wade or even to pray that he would love her the way she wanted him to. What Elyse had said about her had the ring of truth. Why did she find Wade so intriguing?

His air of mystery made him seem out of focus. As in one of Elyse's pictures when someone had moved just before the click of the camera, blurring the image. Wade was a blurred image to Mindy. Who was he really? What did he want from life, from her?

Suddenly Elyse's voice brought Mindy back from her thoughts.

"We're two of a kind, Mindy. Both swimming against the stream in a world that's sometimes hostile—sometimes unforgiving," Elyse added, as if she were remembering some unpleasant or sad experience of the past.

Elyse never really unburdened herself of whatever might have been the cause of her moment of decision. She seemed to have made her peace with an existence that did not include a man, marriage, or a family. Still, she was usually energetic, enthusiastic, and eager. She obviously loved her work. It filled her life, there were no holes she was looking to close with a love affair.

That's why when Wade suddenly came back from one of his unexplained absences, Mindy was almost hesitant to introduce him to Elyse. Was she afraid her perceptive friend would peel away the protective layers that concealed what he was underneath?

Actually, Mindy had been expecting Elyse when the knock came at her parlor door. When she saw Wade, she stood silent for a moment, unbelieving. He had been away this time nearly a month. Now like magic he had reappeared. She had meant to act calm and composed, but the surprise betrayed her and without thinking, she went into the arms he opened.

The embrace, the kisses might have gone on longer except for an obviously cleared throat behind them and Elyse's voice, saying, "Whoops, excuse me. Poor timing. I'll be going—"

Mindy pushed herself out of Wade's arms, flustered. "Oh, Elyse. No, the timing's just right." She laughed self-consciously, patting her loosened hair ineffectively. "Please, come in. This is Wade."

But after being invited in, Elyse stayed only a few minutes then tactfully left saying she had to get up at dawn to photograph the sunrise.

When the door closed behind Elyse, Wade drew Mindy into his arms again, asking, as he always did, "Did you miss me?"

He buried his face in her hair, his lips moved along her temple, her cheek, then covered her mouth with slow, sweet kisses. Then he was holding her tighter and tighter until she couldn't think or breathe, only feel the exciting happiness of his being back.

Chapter 24

Mindy could not wait for Elyse to get to know Wade. So, after that first rather embarrassing incident, she invited her to join them for dinner the following evening. Wade insisted on being their host at the Palace dining room. He was at his charming best, displaying impeccable manners and gave Elyse his undivided attention. He asked her intelligent questions about her work. He offered her his other saddle horse in case she wanted to ride into the desert to take photographs. Mindy, who had been anxious for these two to get along, was pleased that things were going so well.

Since she had confided so much to Elyse about Wade, Mindy was eager to find out what impression he had made on her friend. The next afternoon after work, she stopped by the cottage. Elyse was ready for her questions and did not hesitate to answer them or pose some of her own.

"Handsome, debonair, gracious, a type you don't often see in a rugged frontier town like this. Where's he from?"

"I'm really not sure. He doesn't say much about his background. I have an idea he must be from a wealthy family back east. Maybe the black sheep who came west to prove himself and make a new life," Mindy suggested, adding, "He *does* dress well and is perfectly mannered. . . ."

Elyse half-closed her eyes, as if reminiscing. "Reminds me of a riverboat gambler I met once on a Mississippi paddleboat. Had all the ladies dizzy about him."

Mindy somehow missed the cynicism beneath that remark because she had an impulsive idea she wanted to try on Elyse. "Elyse, would you take a photograph of Wade and me? I'd like to have one to send my mother and brother. I've written to them about him . . . but as you're fond of saying, a picture is worth a thousand words."

Elyse didn't answer right away but went on carefully wrapping her glass plate negatives and placing them into the padded packing boxes. After a minute's pause, she asked warily, "What kind of picture do you have in mind?"

"Oh, just one of us together. Me standing, him sitting, or the other way around. You know best. You told me you've taken dozens of portrait pictures."

"Yes, but I don't anymore. I had my fill of engagement photographs, weddings. I got sick of doing then. They're all so stiff and posed and the couple usually look either scared to death or sick."

"You sound cynical."

"Do I? Sorry. Well, I suppose I am." Elyse still hesitated. "I'm out of sorts today." She paused, hands on her hips facing Mindy. Then she added, "Does Wade want a photo, too?"

"I haven't asked him yet, but I think he will." Mindy's eyes shone. "He's so good looking, I don't think he should be afraid of the camera." She stopped for a second. "But to be honest, it's mostly for me. I'd like to have a picture of us when Wade goes out of town, just to remind me of . . . well, of how marvelous it all is."

"Marvelous?" Elyse repeated. "Are you sure, Mindy, you're not creating castles in Spain?"

"What do you mean? Oh, of course, I know what you mean by castles in Spain." She frowned, "But you mean something else, don't you?"

"I just don't want you to get hurt." Elyse's brow puckered. "Wade doesn't seem to be the kind of man . . . well, I'm afraid you *might* get hurt if you count too much on him."

"For goodness sake, Elyse, I'm not. A picture is all I want, is that too much? You're making a mountain out of a molehill."

"All right," Elyse said, "If that's what you want. I'll do it."

Once that was settled, Mindy made a quick search of her wardrobe for a dress to wear for the sitting. Nothing really seemed right. Wade was always perfectly turned out, and she wanted to look her best. Most of her clothes were serviceable, ones she wore to work, usually covered by a printer's apron. She needed something special to have her picture taken with Wade.

Wade's reaction at first was resistant. "Oh, come on, Mindy, that's nonsense. I'll break Elyse's camera. And that equipment is pretty expensive—she wouldn't appreciate that."

"She's already agreed to do it. Please don't fuss. Elyse'll be leaving soon, and we'll miss this chance. Besides, I want my family to know I'm not making you up." She touched his chin, letting her forefinger slide down the line of his jaw, and teased, "Just to prove that you're real and just as handsome as I told them."

Wade was still unconvinced. "I think it's a lot of foolishness."

Mindy coaxed, "Won't you do it just to please me?"

Reluctantly Wade gave in.

Thrilled that she had talked him into consenting, Mindy took the next step. She had to get something new to wear. She hurried to the town seamstress. Mrs. Farraday had sample dresses she made from patterns she sold. This way a client could see what it looked like made up then have it copied with their own measurements.

Because of Mindy's size, one of the model dresses she tried on fit her perfectly. The seamstress was so surprised, she nearly swallowed the mouthful of pins she had ready to make adjustments if necessary. She stood back, her gaze taking in every inch of Mindy's figure.

"The only problem is this is one of my wedding-dress styles." She eyed Mindy speculatively. "It may be a little too dainty, too fancy for a working woman like yourself, Miss McClaren. Maybe, you want something more . . . well, more—"

"No, I don't think so, Mrs. Faraday. This is really lovely." Mindy smiled at her image in the full-length mirror, turning this way and that.

"Hmm," was Miss Faraday's only comment.

Spontaneously, Mindy said, "Can you keep a secret?"

"I keep plenty, I can tell you. You'd be surprised how many multitudes of sin are covered with material."

Mindy was about to tell her that this dress might someday in the future be used for the purpose it was designed, but before she blurted this out, the seamstress's doorbell rang, interrupting this impulsive confidence. The seamstress hurried to answer it. Two ladies entered, one of whom Mindy recognized as a notorious gossip. This woman always waylaid her when she was on her ad collection rounds and never had a good word to say about anyone. She was certainly not going to reveal anything personal in front of these two.

Even Elyse took a long look at the dress when Mindy showed it to her, asking in a slightly sarcastic tone, "Is there something you're not telling me?"

"Not really. Maybe it's a wishful-thinking kind of dress," Mindy replied dreamily. It was a lovely dress and extremely becoming. She didn't want Elyse to say anything to lower her high spirit. Since Wade's recent return, anything seemed possible.

The day scheduled for the picture-taking session was Friday. The paper would be out, and Mindy would be free until Monday. Elyse was leaving the following Wednesday. The fact that she would be losing her good friend shadowed Mindy's happiness a little as she put on the beautiful dress in preparation of the photographing session set for the afternoon.

When she arrived at the cottage, Elyse took a long hard look at Mindy and affected the local way of showing awe: "Well, if you don't beat all."

"Like it?" Mindy spun around a couple of times. She held out the tiered skirt, touched the puffed sleeves, stretched out her arms showing the lace wrist ruffles.

Elyse put her head to one side. "Are you *sure* you don't have something you're not telling me?"

A quick flush warmed Mindy's cheeks. She tried to sound nonchalant. "It was an impulsive choice, maybe. But every woman ought to have one special dress, shouldn't they?"

"That's usually her wedding dress." Elyse's eyes were serious. "Has the elusive Mr. Carrigan popped the question?"

"Oh, no, nothing like that," Mindy said, changing the subject quickly. Although Wade had not mentioned marriage, they had been so happy together since his return, she had sometimes felt he was on the brink of—proposing?

Yet Mindy had to admit Wade was enigmatic. A few days ago on a picnic, things had never been better. They had talked and laughed and shared. Then suddenly Wade's mood had changed. She couldn't remember now if she had said something that might have triggered it. Had she reminded him of their appointment with Elyse? Whatever, he had turned dead serious. He had put his fingers under her chin and turned her head so she was looking directly at him. "I never thought to have someone like you in my life, Mindy."

"Or I you," she replied, then added, "Aren't we lucky?"

"Some kind of luck. I think you got the worst of the deal."

"Hush, don't say that." She had leaned forward and kissed him. His lips tasted of the cider, sweet, tangy.

They had packed up what was left of the picnic then and ridden home through a glorious sunset.

Elyse's voice brought Mindy sharply back to the present. "Did you tell Wade what time to come?" Elyse was setting up the camera and had arranged an artistic backdrop. She was draping a bench with a velvet cloth.

"Yes. Anything I can do to help?"

"No, I'm about all set," Elyse said looking past her over her shoulder. "Where's Wade?"

"He said he would meet me here. How do I look?"

"Dare I say it? Like a bride."

Mindy laughed, "For heavens sake, don't say that in front of Wade."

"Why not? It might prod him to do the right thing. Anyway it's the truth. I've never seen you look so pretty."

"Then why don't *you* look happy, Elyse?"

"Oh, Mindy, it's just that I'm worried."

"Worried about what?"

"That somehow he's going to break your heart."

"Don't be silly, Elyse, he's not and—"

"Sorry, I shouldn't have said anything." Elyse's mouth tightened and she turned away rearranging the drape again.

"I know you're saying it because you care about me, Elyse, and I appreciate it. But I don't believe Wade would ever hurt me."

"I hope not. Just be careful, Mindy, won't you?"

She gave Mindy an impulsive hug.

"I'm going to miss you, Elyse."

"Don't you dare cry and get your eyes and nose all red before I immortalize you in a photograph," Elyse scolded, and they both laughed.

At fifteen after four, the clock struck the quarter hour. Wade was to have been there at three. Elyse tried not to pointedly consult her watch, but her toe tapped impatiently. Mindy made another futile trip to the window. For the fourth time Mindy said, "I can't imagine where he can be."

At five Elyse remarked, "There's not enough light even if we used oil lamps set all around."

Mindy's heart felt like it was hung with a heavy stone. Why had Wade not come? There must be some explanation.

The explanation came when she checked the livery stable. Wade had taken both of his horses, his saddle bags full, and ridden off to the hills early that morning. He'd left no word when he would be back.

Chapter 25

*T*wo weeks later there still was no explanation for Wade's failing to show up for the scheduled photograph. Even as much as Mindy looked for an excuse, there seemed no reasonable one.

Elyse did not express her own version. Mindy knew her friend was angry for her sake, but she did not want to hear anything against Wade until such time as he would tell her himself. And Mindy was sure that time would come. He would show up. He always did. He jokingly called himself "the bad penny."

She had been terribly disappointed, but she reminded herself that she had made the decision if she loved Wade to take him as he was, not make him measure up to some standard of her own.

Elyse had departed with all her equipment, promising Mindy to keep in touch but already looking forward to her next photographic assignment. This time she hoped it would be to Africa.

Her interesting, stimulating presence gone left a void in Mindy's life and for the first time in quite awhile she felt very lonesome.

Taylor Bradford would have been happy to fill all her free time, but Mindy, aching for the person who was missing, gave him no romantic encouragement. Yet they remained good friends.

For the first time in her young, healthy life Mindy discovered insomnia. Night after night she tossed restlessly, thinking about Wade and wondering why she could not write him off, why she cared so much, why the whole world seemed empty because he was not here. Her work was not enough. At last she realized that. She needed love, an enduring love she could return in full measure.

What had she done wrong? Been too possessive, too open in her own feelings? Had it scared him? In the days that followed Mindy did a great deal of soul searching. About herself, about Wade. He was moody at times, elusive, even secretive. This bothered her truth-seeking soul. Shouldn't people who loved each other share everything?

Another week, then three weeks, passed since he had left. Mindy began to lose confidence. Maybe he had decided their relationship had grown too confining; maybe he wasn't coming back.

Mindy was trying to put thoughts of Wade aside while she readied copy for the Thursday edition, when Taylor walked into the newsroom.

"Howdy, Mindy," he greeted her. "I see you're busy, but I just wondered if you were going to the barbecue Saturday?"

"I don't know for sure. As you can see I've a pile of work here, Taylor." She tapped the pile of copy to be edited with the tip of her pencil.

"Yes, but there's plenty of time. Today's only *Tuesday*, Mindy."

"And tomorrow's Wednesday and the next day's Thursday. The day the paper comes out." She reminded him. "I still have my editorial to write and that always takes some thinking, besides the actual writing."

"Yep, I know." He nodded and grinned. "Hope it ain't about anything that's goin' to upset people."

"No, it's pretty mild this time." She smiled.

"Well, anyhow, if you decide to go, I'd be pleased to escort you."

"Thanks, Taylor, I'll let you know."

She stemmed her impatience to go on with her work, but Taylor was still standing there. "By the way, if you've got room in this week's edition, I'd be obliged if you could print some of these. The deputy from the territory marshal's office just brung 'em over." Taylor laid a stack of WANTED posters at the edge of her desk.

"Sure, Taylor," Mindy replied, wishing he would leave.

However, he wasn't about to pass up the chance to talk to Mindy when she was not surrounded by other people. "It's amazin' how often a criminal can walk around a town unnoticed till someone sees his picture on one of these and turns him in."

Mindy nodded and tried not to let her impatience show.

Taylor hesitated, and she could tell he had something more he wanted to say.

"About the barbecue, after all, it's the Fourth of July, Mindy."

Fourth of July! Her birthday, Mindy realized with a start.

She had kept so busy and so preoccupied with her worries about Wade, she had almost forgotten. She would be twenty-four.

"It's a holiday. You shouldn't work on a holiday," Taylor said.

"Yes, you're right. I'll see what I can do, and well, thank you for reminding me, Taylor. As I said I'll let you know." She didn't want to promise anything. Maybe—just maybe—Wade would show up.

After Taylor finally left Mindy went right to work on her editorial. She definitely wanted that done if Wade *did* arrive. Writing it took her less time than usual. Nothing controversial this week, thank goodness. That done, she went quickly through the rest of the material for this edition. The paper would be put to bed tomorrow when Pete came in to set the rest of the type. She stacked the copy to be typeset, then picked up the pile of posters Taylor had left to see which ones to include this week.

Suddenly, her fingers holding one of the WANTED posters went numb. She stared at the picture in stunned disbelief. The image was blurred, as if there had been too much ink on the roller, yet there was something undeniably recognizable about that face . . . something devastatingly familiar. It couldn't be. *Wanted for bank robberies in three states, Missouri, Kansas, Oklahoma.* Calvin Warner, alias Cary Wadener, Warren Clay.

Mindy sat perfectly still at her desk as if turned to stone. A fly buzzed noisily in the corner of the dusty window through which the late afternoon sunlight streamed. As though it came from a long distance away, she heard the sound of the anvil at the blacksmith shop down the street, a wagon rumbled by, a dog barked, two men greeted each other loudly outside the newspaper office.

She shivered as if icy water were pouring through her veins. Her hands began to shake. No, it couldn't be—and yet she knew it was. Although the picture was crude, it was undeniably Wade. She knew that face; she had traced her finger along the brows over those eyes staring so defiantly out of that photograph; she had stroked that strong jaw line and kissed that mouth.

Sick and miserable, full of pain, somehow she managed to close up the office and walk unseeingly down the street home. She had to tell someone and yet, wouldn't that betray Wade? Should she tell Taylor? He must not have looked through this batch of posters before he had brought them to her. Or did he know? Did he want to see if she would act upon the values declared so strongly in her editorials:

integrity, truthfulness, principles to build a better community? Was he testing her?

The need to confide what she suspected—no, what she had *found out* was great. But there was no one she could trust with this information without revealing her own interest in him. Elyse was gone. She had no one to ask what she should do. She was bound to report what she knew to be the truth. A bank robber masquerading as a law-abiding citizen in their midst. Wade.

Stiffly, as though walking in a trance, Mindy went to her rooms. Her mind was in turmoil. Where was Wade now? At his mine site—or his *so-called* mine site? Was that a lie too? How many lies had he told? How many had she believed? Mindy went into her bedroom and closed the door behind her. Her breath was coming in choking gulps. Ragged sobs welled up from deep within. How could she have been so misled? Her gaze fell on the water-silk dress hanging outside her wardrobe. Hot tears rushed into her eyes. The dress she thought might be her wedding gown. How ironic! How she had been fooled! By his charm, by his devious charm. Mindy flung herself face down on the bed and wept.

Exhausted, she finally cried herself out. She sat up, her head pounding, and tried to think through Wade's horrible secret. How long had he thought he could get away with concealing his identity? Colorado was a long way from Missouri and Kansas and yet there was telegraph and the railroad connecting the country, and people traveled nowadays and brought news from other parts. And what was he doing on these mysterious trips? Were there other bank robberies closer at hand? Did he work alone? Or was he one of a band of outlaws? Her mind would only go so far along these paths. She could not associate the Wade she knew with the action of a wanted bank robber. She had known the comfort of his embrace, the ecstasy of his kisses. She had loved him—did she still love him? Or could a person love a stranger? Because that's what Wade seemed now. Someone she didn't know.

What would she say, what would she do when she saw him? *God only knows,* she thought, and it was a prayer.

She slept hardly at all. Finally, sometime before dawn, she threw herself across her bed and fell into an exhausted shallow sleep. Awakening scant hours later, when day was breaking, she dragged herself up. She had to go back to the newspaper and do what had to be done.

She unlocked the door to the building and let herself in. Pete and Timmy wouldn't be in until later. She was glad. She needed time to be alone. The place smelled strongly of ink, machine oil, and scorched coffee. Checking, she found she had left the coffee pot on the stove and the remains in it had burned away.

Mindy went to her desk, moved the pile of papers from one side to the other, and sat down. She put her elbows on the surface, her chin on her fists, and sat there staring at nothing. Nothing registered, but the agonizing pain that had wrung her out emotionally throughout the long hours of the night was still lodged so heavily in her chest that she could hardly draw a deep breath.

Through the front window she saw Main Street, its early morning traffic moving in front of her unseeing eyes. Her mind had blocked out everything but the inevitable question. What was she to do about the poster she was now convinced was Wade?

She never knew how long she sat there when the door opened with its usual creak and she heard his voice: "Penny for your thoughts, lady."

She blinked and jumped. Wade! He walked in with his assured saunter, clean-shaven, immaculately groomed, perfectly at ease. "What's the matter?" he teased. "Cat got your tongue?"

He seemed on top of the world, his pockets full of cash. *Other people's money.* He had on a brand new broadcloth coat, a crisp ruffled shirt, gold cufflinks glinted as he pulled up a chair and sat down with languid grace. "And have you been slaving here all weekend, my darling?" he asked her. "You look quite weary. You shouldn't work so hard. Not good for you. Unless—is there some big story breaking?"

"As a matter of fact there just may be," she replied with stiff lips, thinking, *How can he be so calm, so nonchalant?*

"Oh?" He raised his eyebrows.

"Why don't *you* tell *me*, Wade? Or is it Cary or Warren?" She hadn't meant to blurt it all out like that, it just happened.

Something flickered in his eyes regarding her. There was a moment of absolute silence. Then he said slowly, "How did you find out?"

So he wasn't going to deny it. He wouldn't even try to pretend indignation or declare he was being falsely accused. Mindy was taken aback. She did not know what she had expected, but it wasn't this casual agreement.

She took the poster from the bottom of the pile she had stuffed in the drawer of the desk and held it up to him.

"Not a very good likeness. I'm surprised you recognized it," he commented dryly.

"I've studied your face a good deal," she said quietly. Now, it was out in the open. Nothing held back but the truth all these months.

"So you have. And I yours. I love you, Mindy. Don't forget that."

"Then why this? Why all the lies ... how can I believe anything when you never told me the truth about yourself."

"The reasons I never told you should be obvious." He flung out both hands. "What you saw was what you got. What you imagined was your own."

"But—"

"No, Mindy, you pride yourself on being honest, and a good reporter, as well." His mouth twisted sardonically. "Did you ask me any questions about my life, my past? You believed what you wanted to believe."

"But what about your mine, your partner?"

"All true. It just doesn't happen to pay as well as . . . shall we say, some other of my enterprises."

She gazed at him aghast. Didn't his conscience bother him? "But I loved you." Even to herself, her voice sounded whining and she hated it.

"And this makes you not love me?"

"I have to respect the person I love. How can I respect a thief?" The words came out bitterly.

"'Love is not love that alters when it alteration finds.' You've heard that, haven't you? Love means loving that person no matter what. Not respect, nor the so-called virtues. Love is love, a blind, irrational emotion." He got slowly to his feet. "If you love me, Mindy, you'll accept who I am, not what you want me to be."

She shook her head, "I can't. I can't love someone who defies the very things I honor most."

"I can't be all that. It's up to you, Mindy." He paused, "Does Taylor know?"

"No, not yet. He just brought in this batch of posters, asked me to print how ever many I had room for."

Wade's eyebrows went up, "And did you?"

"Not yet—"

"Well, now you know. What are you going to do?"

She drew a long breath. "I'll give you twenty-four hours to turn yourself in, Wade."

"You trust me to do that?"

"I want to, I hope so. I don't want to be totally wrong about you."

Wade smiled or at least the corners of his mouth lifted. But there was no humor in the smile, no tenderness in his eyes as he regarded her.

"It's a gambler's world, Mindy. The luck of the draw. We happened to be in the same town, at the same time, one of those strange chances in life. Everyone has to play the hand they're dealt. You, yours; me, mine."

Words rushed into Mindy's mind to say—pleas, bargains. But she knew they were futile. Wherever Wade had learned his code of ethics, they were a far cry from hers. The values she held he considered unimportant. He made his own rules. And they broke all hers.

She thought love could change him. She had been wrong. Something stronger than her love led him to whatever uncertain destiny was his. What that might be made her afraid for him.

"You're quite a woman, Mindy. In a way, I wish I deserved you."

There was such finality in the way he spoke, Mindy knew what he planned to do. She had promised to give him twenty-four hours to give himself up. He would use those hours to save himself. In the twenty-four hours reprieve she had given him, he would be far away from Coarse Gold. This was the end.

She swung her chair around and stood. Wade rose too. He took a tentative step toward her to take her into his arms and kiss her for one last time. Then he halted. His gaze swept over her as if he were memorizing her. Then he put on his hat and walked to the door. He stopped there, turned, tipped his hat, and then went out.

The sound of the door clicking shut moved her to action. As she ran after him, his name caught in her throat. She reached the door, flung it open, and stood there looking out into the street. She stood motionless, watching him swing gracefully onto his horse, then without turning to look back, he rode down Main Street. At the corner, he broke into a canter and disappeared in the early morning mist.

She fought a terrible sense of desolation and loss. However, Mindy realized she had had no other choice.

She gathered up the batch of posters and walked over to Taylor's office. He looked up in surprise at her entrance, pushed back his chair and stood up.

"Why, Miss Mindy, this is an unexpected pleasure."

"It's no pleasure, Taylor, and no social visit, I'm afraid." She put the posters face down on his desk. "I don't know if you had a chance to go through these before you brought them over to the paper, but I think you best do it now. Carefully."

Taylor glanced at her hard. "Something's wrong, isn't it? You look—" With one hand he shoved one of the chairs toward her. "Please, sit down."

She shook her head. "No thank you, Taylor. I can't. I've had a shock that's all. I just need a little time to get over it." She turned and walked back over to the door. "I didn't print any of these in this week's edition. What goes into the newspaper is the editor's personal decision. But you have a job to do. I understand that." Her throat was tightening up as she spoke. She knew she had to get out of here before she broke down.

"I'm sorry, Miss Mindy." Taylor said not knowing why he was offering her sympathy or what for.

Mindy simply nodded and went out the door. Blinded by tears she somehow made her way down the street to Mrs. Busby's. All she could think of was to escape from this nightmare of broken dreams.

Chapter 26

or Mindy, the next few weeks dragged by in a kind of monotonous grayness. The paper got out, but sometimes she did not even remember how. She was aware that the brassy heat of late summer had come and gone, merging into the mellow coolness of autumn. She drove herself relentlessly, going into the newspaper office early and staying late. She wanted to be so tired at the end of the day that she could not think; she just wanted to fall into bed, hoping for the oblivion of sleep.

She thought she had made progress from the heartbreaking discovery of Wade's identity. How close to the surface all her emotions were she did not realize until late one sultry afternoon Taylor walked into the office. His clothes were dusty and Mindy belatedly remembered he had been gone out of town for a few days. By the look of him he had come straight from the saddle to the newspaper. He looked uncomfortable, and a tingle of alarm went all through Mindy. Somehow she knew Taylor had some bad news to tell her. Without bothering to greet him she asked, "What is it?"

"It's about Wade Carrigan," he said, approaching her desk. He took off his sweat stained hat and thrust a hand through his uncombed hair. I thought you'd want to know. We've brought him in, my deputy's just locked him up in our jail."

"How did it . . . where did you . . . ?" Mindy's lips were stiff as she tried to form the words.

"On a hunch, actually. We wuz ridin' back from Silver Creek, and we decided to branch off up the canyon, and we come on the place where he and his gang stashed their loot. It was in an old silver mine." He paused, twisting his hat. "You know how he used to talk about him and his partner having a mine . . . well that was it. Only it weren't silver they had there, it was gold bars, twenty dollar gold pieces, you name it, they had it. They run a pretty successful operation. We surprised 'em, don't know what they wuz plannin', but we caught 'em red-handed, so to speak."

"Now what?"

"Well, we've got to notify the marshal over to Boulder. He's wanted in three states 'sides Colorado."

"Anyone hurt? I mean was there shooting?"

"Nah, not so you could speak of. We snuck up on 'em. They was all asleep. We spooked their horses a little, but even that didn't wake them all the way. There was the three of us and two of them. It were pretty easy."

"So, they'll stay here until . . ."

"We'll have to escort them over to Boulder where they'll stand trial, make sure they don't get away. They're a slick bunch, all right." He shifted from one foot to the other. "I just thought I ought tell you myself."

Mindy knew Taylor had some idea how strong her feelings were for Wade. It had stung him that she had chosen Wade over him. Now, he seemed uncomfortable at the way things had turned out, as if she might hold it against him that he had been the one to bring Wade in. Mindy hastened to reassure him.

"Good work, Sheriff."

Taylor shook his head, "Durndest thing, not that I ever knew him all that well. But he appeared to be a sure enough nice fella. Polite for all that. But you know, Mindy . . ." Taylor squinted his eyes as if reliving the scene. "That time over at Silver Creek when I hit that robber running out of the bank in the leg and one of his partners turned his gun on me, I thought, I could have been mistook, but, even then the thought come to me there was something familiar about him. His face was shaded by his hat brim but there was something, I dunno what, the set of his shoulders when he turned in his saddle—something made me think I'd seen him somewheres before." Taylor rubbed his wrist reflectively. "I know he was a durn good shot."

Mindy made no comment. What could she say? Now that it was all out. Wade, who had eluded capture for years, arrested by Taylor and locked in the Coarse Gold jail. It was when all these facts hit that Mindy's blood began to stir, setting in motion the possibility that had not occurred to her at first. Her pulse began to race.

"Can I see him?"

Taylor's eyes widened. "You mean *visit* him? In the jail?"

"Taylor, this is a big story. It will put Coarse Gold and its sheriff on the map."

"What do you mean?"

"I'd like to get his story for the *Gazette*. I want an interview. Wade's wanted in three states. Papers in all three will fight for this story. I want to get it first. Eastern papers go wild over true-life western stories—shootouts, stage coach robberies, outlaws, brave lawmen."

Taylor was hesitant. He shifted uneasily. "I don't know, Mindy."

Mindy stood up, buttoned her jacket, put on her bonnet, and picked up her notebook and two sharpened pencils.

"This will surely be picked up by newspapers in Sacramento, San Francisco—you'll be a hero, Taylor. It's important that we get the facts right. I'll do a good job, I promise."

"Well, all right, but you're not going in the cell. Outside only, and my deputy sitting there with his shotgun while you do the interview." He paused. "What if Wade won't talk, don't want to be interviewed?"

"Oh, I think he will," Mindy said and walked to the door.

Her back straight, shoulders back, her notebook clutched tightly, Mindy gave all the appearance of outward calm. Inside, her stomach churned to see Wade in such circumstances. She had to look composed, not show a trace of emotion. This *was* a big story. A one-on-one, face-to-face interview with a notorious bank robber.

Taylor gave the order to his deputy to unlock the door to the prisoners' cells. The young man glanced at Mindy open-mouthed, then back at Taylor again for confirmation. Taylor nodded, and he took out a ring of keys and opened the door leading to the jail section back of the sheriff's office.

Mindy took a deep breath and started through. Behind her she heard the sound of the deputy's boots loud on the bare floor, the spurs jangling, as he followed her.

As she entered the area with four cramped barred cells, Wade looked up from where he was half-lounging on a narrow cot. When he saw her, his expression was unreadable. Surprise, puzzlement, shame? Mindy thought she saw all three pass over his unshaven face. Then he smiled that old familiar smile that used to rock her heart and slowly rose to his feet, tucking in the tails of his rumpled shirt.

Several days stubble of beard was dark on his lean-jawed face. She had never seen Wade less than perfectly groomed. Now he looked disheveled, haggard.

"Well, if it isn't the editor of the *Roaring River Gazette*. Such an unexpected pleasure. What brings you here?" There was amusement and curiosity in his glance.

"I'm here to get your story."

"I thought you might be on a mission of mercy. Sent by the Ladies Benevolent Society to minister to the wretched prisoner."

"No. You're page-one material."

"Ah, so that's it."

The deputy pushed a straight chair forward, in front of the cell, and Mindy sat down. Wade took a few steps forward, placed both hands on the bars, and leaned against them.

Mindy avoided looking at him directly. Her fingers gripped the pencil poised over her notebook.

"I'd like to ask you a few questions."

"Well what do you want to know?"

She wanted to know so much. Everything. How it had all come down to this. The where, when, how, and why. Mostly the Why. All the other questions flew out of her mind and she blurted out. "Why?"

"Why?" He repeated. "Why I chose a life of crime? Why not a banker but a bank robber?" His tone was sarcastic. "You want to know why. Maybe because I like taking risks, the gamble, the challenge to get away with it. Play the game and not get caught. Outrun the posse. Make a laughing stock of the law. Out smart them all."

"But you're capable of so much more—"

"How do you know that?" His mouth twisted sardonically. "You really don't know much about me."

"Then tell me so I can understand."

He hesitated, then, "Shall we begin at the beginning? When I was a skinny little kid? I had an older brother—my father's favorite. Brad could do no wrong. He was killed in an accident. Fording a river that was actually too deep to risk it, but he always went for the toughest things. It was swollen by floods, but he took the chance he could make it. His horse stumbled and fell. Brad's foot was caught in the stirrup, the horse rolled over on him, and he was drowned. It nearly killed my father, too. He never got over Brad's dying. He turned on everything. Me included. He'd say, 'Be a man, like your brother.' To me, at ten years old. In his view, the way to prove you were a man was never to turn down a dare, do the reckless, most dangerous thing. Hah, I

212

grew up under that taunt. When the war broke out, to show my father, I enlisted. I was only fifteen. I lied about my age to get in the army. The first of many lies." Wade shook his head. "When Lee surrendered, my captain wouldn't and made us swear we'd never accept defeat or amnesty. So we formed a renegade group, and we came west."

"And when you came west?"

"We broke up into small groups," he shrugged. "That's how it really began. The war had robbed me of everything. Our farm was burned by bushwhackers, my mother died, then my father and I had nothing to go back to. I had to make my own life. Be a man. The only way I knew to do that—well, was do things I thought my father would admire."

"Then you have no remorse?" Wade gave Mindy a long look. "None for all the people you hurt, the money that didn't belong to you, for all the lies you told? The silver you were supposed to have?"

"The mine was a front. So I could have somewhat of a normal life between—" His lips parted in a half-grin. "—between jobs."

She wrote a big question mark so hard the pencil post snapped.

"As for the lies, sure, there were plenty of those, my whole life was a lie, I made it up as I went along." Wade leaned forward, lowering his voice, "The only time I didn't lie, Mindy, was when I told you I loved you."

I won't listen to any more, Mindy told herself, and stood up. "Is there anything else you want to add to the account?"

"I'm sure you can fill in the blanks. I'll give you your headline. 'Unrepentant, unreconstructed Rebel squanders life, lives high on the hog on stolen money.'" Wade gave a harsh laugh. "You're a good writer, Mindy, I can count on you to write a whoppin' good story. Sell a lot of newspapers."

Disconcerted, Mindy pushed back the chair. The deputy behind her stood up. "Then, I guess that's all unless . . . shall we say you have no regrets?"

"A final word, Mindy, I do have a regret, my only regret. But then you probably know what that is."

Back at her desk, Mindy was trembling. But she was satisfied that she had lived up to her highest standards of professional behavior. She had not allowed her personal feelings to prevent her getting an important story. Byron would have been proud of her. "To thine own self be true."

She reread the few notes she had taken. While Wade was talking, she sometimes pretended to be writing but was actually too moved by what he was saying to put it down. What he had told her she would never forget. If only he had told her some of this sooner . . . maybe she could have helped him, maybe things could have been different.

But down deep she knew no one can save another person from himself. That was humanly impossible. "But with God anything is possible." During the long-term sentence he would probably get for the many robberies, Wade would have time to think about his life, search his soul. All she could do now was pray for him.

Sighing, Mindy began to write. An hour later, she put the copy on Pete's desk with the instruction "Set in banner headlines: NOTORIOUS BANK ROBBER ARRESTED BY LOCAL SHERIFF."

Chapter 27

*I*n the weeks following Wade's arrest, Mindy had difficulty dealing with the callousness revealed in the interview. How could she have been so deceived? She blamed herself for ignoring some of the signs she should have noticed, the ones Elyse saw and had now certainly turned out to be true. What a waste of a brilliant mind, a man of physical strength and many abilities.

Determined to not let her disillusionment with Wade destroy or embitter her, Mindy reminded herself she had a great deal to be thankful for: work she loved, her youth, her health. Gradually, as the months went by, the wounds caused by Wade's betrayal began to heal. As she rebounded from disappointment and disillusion, she discovered she was stronger than she had thought. Her natural optimism resurfaced and she found she could look to the future with hope.

Then one day a letter, postmarked Sacramento, arrived.

My dear Miss McClaren,
  I am about to complete my business here and am planning to come to Coarse Gold within the next week. I will

again be on a mission for my mother. She was grieved that there was no headstone on Uncle Byron's grave and has asked me to arrange for one to be placed there with an appropriate epitaph.

May I prevail on your kindness and affection for my uncle to help me select one? Mother and I agree that you would be the person most able to do this. You knew him so well during the years when we, his family, did not have the opportunity to be with him.

If it is still available and convenient for me to do so, may I stay in Uncle Byron's cottage? This will give me ample time to go more thoroughly through his belongings, making decisions about what to keep and what should be disposed of or packed and shipped to Pennsylvania. I may also ask you assistance in these matters as well.

I sincerely hope I am not imposing on our short acquaintance by asking you these favors. I did so enjoy the time we spent together on my last trip. I look forward to seeing you soon.

Yours,

Lawrence Day

Mindy was delighted to learn Byron's nephew was coming back to Coarse Gold. She had very much enjoyed his company, his thoughtful comments, and his stimulating conversation.

She had become a virtual recluse since the whole unhappy situation with Wade. The *Gazette* had become the entire focus of her life, and she knew that was not good. Even so, she was surprised at how glad she was to see Lawrence Day when he walked into the newspaper office the following week.

She had also forgotten how much he reminded her of Byron. Not so much in appearance, because Lawrence was actually a very handsome young man, but more in his mannerisms, the way he always seemed to give thoughtful consideration to his answers to questions, and most of all, how his smile and laugh were genuine and spontaneous.

Mindy walked with him to Byron's cottage, which she had had cleaned and aired in preparation for his stay. "You are so kind, Miss McClaren, to make everything so comfortable and easy for me. But—" He glanced around the front room. "—I am at a loss as to what to do with all of this? I may need more of your help, look at all these books ... I don't suppose—Coarse Gold doesn't have a lending library?" He shot a hopeful glance at Mindy who shook her head.

"No, I'm sorry it doesn't. I've often thought someone should start one. I must confess I've sometimes come over here and borrowed a few of Byron's. He was always urging his favorites on me." "I can see I've my work cut out for me," Lawrence said with a rueful smile. "But I can take the time on this trip. I plan to stay until I've accomplished what I've come to do."

Mindy started to the door, "Well, I'll leave you to it, then."

"Oh, Miss McClaren, would you have dinner with me tonight ... at the inestimable Mrs. Busby's? I still yearn for more of her chicken and dumplings."

"She'll be thrilled to hear that, and yes, I would like to have dinner with you. Thank you."

That evening was one of the most interesting, stimulating ones Mindy had had in months.

At dinner, their conversation turned to other things. Lawrence was very knowledgeable about many things, and Mindy realized that she was unaware of the progress of life outside this backwater town—for example, new trends in the newspaper publishing business.

"Newspapers back east are changing rapidly, making old methods obsolete. Have you heard of the linotype machine?" he asked Mindy.

"No, what is it?"

"It was invented by a man named Ottmar Mergenthaler. To operate it, a man sits in front of the machine and types out the copy. Then, at the end of each line, he pulls a level, and the entire line of type is cast in hot lead right then and

217

there, and dropped into place. It saves having to set every-thing by hand."

"But what about printers? Doesn't that put printers out of a job?" She thought of Pete who was nearing sixty. Could he learn a new skill at his age if by some stretch of the imagination the *Gazette* could get one of these machines.

"Printers would welcome it, I should think. It would make their work much easier. More type set faster. It would improve the speed at which you could get a paper out. You'd be able to print more stories each issue, fill the paper with more advertising, make it more attractive."

"I suppose they're expensive."

"They are now, but I'm certain the price will go down as soon as the demand increases. It would eventually pay for itself in saved time and more revenue from advertisers."

"That sounds very exciting, but in a small town news-paper, I wonder if it would be cost effective?"

"Why not? The west is where everything will be hap-pening in the next few years. A newspaper is the hub and heartbeat of a town. A town has a special relationship to its newspaper." He smiled at Mindy. "And to its editor."

"I worry about the older printers though," Mindy said doubtfully. "It would be hard for them to learn a new trade."

"For some, yes, but for others maybe not. And there will be young men coming up looking for a trade, something interesting, challenging. I believe trade schools will be established to teach how to use the linotype. It's going to revolutionize newspaper printing."

As their dinner of pot roast, vegetables, potatoes, and gravy was served, they talked of other things. Lawrence told Mindy he was looking forward to his task at his uncle's house.

The evening ended with Lawrence seeing Mindy to her parlor door. They agreed to meet the next day when Mindy would take him to see Elton Lockman, the stone cutter.

Still stimulated by this evening of unusual and interesting companionship and conversation, Mindy found it hard to settle down. So instead of going directly to bed, she looked through some of her source books and her Bible, searching for just the right quotation for Byron's epitaph. Of course, this would be subject to his nephew's approval.

It was more difficult than she had imagined. Byron would have hated anything false—an expression of a piety he did not profess, a virtue he did not posses, a strength or quality he had not attained.

Finally, yawning, Mindy gave up her search. Perhaps Lawrence would discover something suitable. They could discuss it tomorrow or some other day while he was here.

They met as planned for breakfast where Mindy confessed her failure to find the perfect epitaph. "I'm sorry, Mr. Day, I haven't yet found exactly the right one."

"There's no hurry. I have no pressing date to return home. I'm grateful for your allowing me to stay in Uncle Byron's cottage. It's true what people say that a house reflects its occupant's personality and character. I'm learning a great deal I never knew about my uncle. He loved the classics. He has many books about music and art."

As they started out to walk to the stonecutter's, Lawrence said, "May I ask you one more favor?"

"Of course."

"Would you call me 'Lawrence'? 'Mr. Day' sounds so formal."

"Of course," she smiled, "and since your uncle sometimes called me 'McClaren' and at other times 'Mindy,' I think the privilege could be extended to his nearest of kin."

Lockman, the stonecutter, was a thin, wiry man with perennially stooped shoulders. His bald head, beard, and clothing were finely drifted with white stone dust. When Mindy introduced him to Lawrence, Lockman expressed his pleasure: "I liked your uncle. He had an eye for beauty. He used to come and look at my stones. Funny, he didn't pick out one for himself."

They wandered about the yard outside the small work-shop, and Lockman showed them different varieties of stone and granite.

"How much you fixin' to say on the headstone?"

Lawrence looked at Mindy. "We haven't quite decided yet. How long does it usually take to carve an epitaph?"

"Depends on how much you want to say," was the laconic reply.

"Naturally. I'll give you his full name, date of birth, death, right away so you can get started, then as soon as we make that decision, we'll let you know. I'd like to have it done and set in place before I go back east."

Lawrence and Mindy had dinner together again that evening, and afterwards, Mindy invited Lawrence into her parlor so they could search through some of her books to find the right epitaph. For three successive evenings they repeated the same routine. After much exchange of ideas, much reading out loud to each other of quotations they found in their individual search, they finally decided on the choice of quotation for the headstone.

On Friday, after the paper was put to bed, they met and went out to the stonecutter's again. Lawrence handed Lockman the slip of paper on which the epitaph was printed, and they exchanged the possible dates for completing the carving. When Lawrence told Lockman he planned to leave by the end of the month, the stonecutter promised to begin it right away.

Mindy was startled at the sharp pang of regret she felt at the thought of Lawrence leaving. When he left she would probably never see him again. He had been such an inter-esting companion these last two weeks she knew it would be hard to be on her own again.

The day the stonecutter sent the message that the headstone was ready, they went together to see it. It had turned out beautifully. The pale gray granite was the perfect background for the words. TO THINE OWN SELF BE TRUE, THOU CANST NOT THEN BE FALSE TO ANY MAN, followed by his name and the dates of his birth and death.

"He tried to live that, and he allowed other people that privilege as well," Mindy said softly, recalling how many times Byron had turned her questions around saying, "Well, what do *you* think about that yourself?" He gave her credit for having some intelligence, even opinions that might be opposite to his own.

The next step was to arrange with the minister to dedicate the grave when the headstone was placed. Coincidentally, they met the Reverend Thompson on their way back to the newspaper office, and he said he'd be happy to conduct a graveside service the following Sunday afternoon. That was only three days away. After that, Mindy realized, Lawrence would probably have to go back east, and her life would seem empty again.

She would miss him terribly. Since Elyse Sinclair had left, Mindy had no one to really talk to until Lawrence had come. His intellect had sharpened her own. He brought up interesting subjects, widened her insights, opened her understanding about what was happening in the west. She realized there would be a void in her life when he left.

One thing that drew her to him was that he had so many of the same qualities she had admired in Byron—but none of the fatal flaws. Lawrence was a gentleman in every respect without being the least bit weak. He was knowledgeable without being dogmatic, consistent in his ideas without being opinionated, strong without being domineering. He was as ideal in character as anyone she had ever met. She felt unhappy that when he left Coarse Gold, she probably would never see him again.

On Friday the last week in September, Mindy sat at her desk pondering her life. The paper was published, and usually Mindy felt a deep sense of accomplishment—gratified that the *Gazette* had come out for another week, that somehow she had managed to pull it off once more.

But somehow, this Friday, Mindy was overwhelmed with a sense of loneliness and futility. Why? Didn't she have what she wanted? Actually, more than she had ever imagined possible—a newspaper of her own. Hadn't she been given the respect and recognition she had yearned for? Why, then, this feeling of emptiness?

Down deep she knew Lawrence's pending departure depressed her. He had put it off for the logical excuse of his uncle's memorial service. Now, that was over and still he had not made definite plans to leave.

Mindy couldn't seem to settle down. She tried straightening the clutter on her desk but she mostly ended up holding a batch of papers uncertainly and staring into space.

Her thoughts were still in a muddle when the door opened, and Lawrence walked into the newsroom. It was as if her thoughts had somehow wished him here.

"Finished for the day? If you are, would you like to walk up to the cemetery with me? I'd like to pay my last respects to Uncle Byron."

"Yes, I'd like that." Mindy quickly scooped up the scattered papers, stuffed them into her wire IN basket, and snatched her bonnet and shawl off the coat tree. "Shall we go?"

When they started out it was still warm but there was a tinge of autumn in the air. The weather was cooler now in the mornings, and soon the days would grow shorter. The sky was a cloudless blue. As they mounted the hill to the graveyard, Mindy could hear meadowlarks singing. It was beautiful, yet it somehow made her feel melancholy.

At the crest, they turned to look back at the town. It was growing day by day. They could see the scaffolding of another set of buildings at the lower end of Main Street.

More people arrived every week, and not just miners, but those who wanted to set up shop or open a business. The newspaper subscription list was also growing, and advertisers followed in a steady stream.

For all that this past year had brought, life in Coarse Gold had been good to her. Mindy felt that people respected her and liked her. She had found a place here. Why, then, was she conscious of a nagging unmet need? Why, after all she had done, was there still some intangible longing in her heart she could not even name? A sense of incompleteness, a yearning for something she could not quite define?

Wordlessly, they turned back and continued up the rise. When they were almost to the top Lawrence halted and looked at Mindy. "Maybe this isn't the right time or place, but, Mindy, I have to ask you a question. I'm willing to accept whatever your answer is, and I apologize beforehand if I am stepping over the line in this."

Suddenly Mindy felt a breathlessness she knew wasn't due to the exertion of the climb.

"I want you to know that coming to know you has been one of the nicest things that has ever happened to me." He smiled. "I came to Coarse Gold as a favor to my mother. To carry out her request about Uncle Byron's grave." He gestured toward the cemetery. "However, I've found something totally unexpected, something very valuable. Our friendship."

Friendship. She considered his choice of words.

"At least, that's what I've been telling myself. But, when I've been honest with myself, it is far more than that. What I have to say is that *for me*, it has gone beyond that." He paused. "Mindy, I have come to care for you deeply."

He waited, as if hoping for encouragement from her to go on. But Mindy only stared at him speechless. "If this, in any way, disturbs you, I'll go no further."

She shook her head.

He reached for her hand, held it up, examining it. Her hands were small and square and capable. "I love you, Mindy." His fingers circled the third finger of her left hand, "I'd like to place a wedding ring on this one."

Mindy looked into his eyes that searched hers. His declaration was so unexpected she was at a loss. Was what she felt for Lawrence truly love or just the fear of loneliness? The loneliness that she dreaded would overtake her after he left? She didn't know. She wasn't sure.

With her free hand she brushed back a stray strand of hair, and Lawrence took one of her hairpins that had come loose and replaced it. It was such a gently intimate gesture, Mindy felt her heart turn over.

He was regarding her with such tenderness. How could she answer? "To thine own self be true" came into Mindy's mind. How many times Byron had quoted that to her. A dozen possibilities came into Mindy's mind. Reasons to say yes, reasons to say no. Reasons that his next words strengthened.

"I would love to take you back to Pennsylvania with me. To meet my mother and see the house I built. I didn't know it at the time but it was meant for you, Mindy. It has lots of windows, and it looks out on the woodland that stretches all the way to the river. You can see the falls from it, and on summer nights, when it is very quiet, you can hear the sound of it. Oh, Mindy, I know you'd love it." He reached and took her hand, brought it to his lips and kissed it. "Please say, you'll come. You won't regret it, I promise. I'll spend my life making you happy."

Mindy's throat tightened. She longed to say yes to him. He had all the qualities she could ever hope for in a man. And he loved her, was offering her his world to share.

But what about *her* world here in Coarse Gold? What would happen to the paper? Could she give up all she had worked so hard to achieve? If she followed the emotional desire of her heart for love, protection, and security, it would mean—leaving Colorado. Going back east to Lawrence's hometown would mean a total change from the life she had here. What kind of life would that be? What would Lawrence expect of her? The traditional role of a supportive wife beside her husband?

Lawrence was the kindest, most gentle, and most considerate person she had ever known. But was that enough? To give up her hard-earned independence, her freedom? Impossible.

"You don't have to make up your mind right away, Mindy," Lawrence said. "I know it's a big decision to make. An important one. All I can say, is that I love you very much."

"Thank you, Lawrence. I'm flattered by what you've said. But, yes, I need time. So much to think about ..." Her voice trailed off uncertainly.

"I understand. I won't pressure you." Still holding her hand they continued up the hill.

Meanwhile Mindy prayed fervently. *If this is your Will for me, Lord. Show me. Give me a sign.* She had been taught it was wrong to bargain with God, but she felt so shaky, so unsure, the decision was such a big one, she needed guidance. Divine guidance.

Together they stood at Byron's grave. Mindy read the engraving and knew she had received her sign, her answer. TO THINE OWN SELF BE TRUE, THOU CANST NOT THEN BE FALSE TO ANY MAN.

If she left Coarse Gold now, she would be betraying herself. She had come too far, worked too hard, accomplished too much to leave it all behind. It would not be fair to herself. More important, it would not be fair to Lawrence. She remembered what Elyse had said about both herself and Mindy. They were a different kind of woman. If she accepted Lawrence's proposal, how long would such happiness satisfy her? A part of herself would always be denied. He was too fine a person to give him a divided heart.

So Mindy gave Lawrence her answer. Even the night before he was to leave, he attempted a last-ditch plea to get her to change her mind and to come with him. "I promise you, I won't try to change you, won't try to force you into some kind of mold. I love you the way you are, Mindy. I love everything about you. Why would I do anything to alter that?"

All his arguments were in vain. Mindy felt she had received her direction. She was to stay in Coarse Gold, convinced it was God's will for her life, determined to fulfill that destiny.

She knew Lawrence was leaving on the noon stage to Boulder. Then he'd catch the train back east. She stayed busy working at her desk, trying not to look up from the copy she was editing to look out the window. From her desk she had a direct view of Main Street and the Palace Hotel where the stagecoach took on passengers. She dared not look, afraid she might see him, and lose all her resolve, to dash out there.

And do what? Beg him not to go? Or worse, throw caution to the winds and agree to go with him? Mindy pressed her mouth into a tight line and kept working.

However, she couldn't miss the shouts of the driver and his helper as they loaded on the luggage. Then she heard the crack of his whip, the jangle of the horses harnesses, the creak of the wheels as the coach started off. In spite of herself, Mindy jumped up from her desk and ran through the newsroom, pushed open the door, then stood there watching as the stagecoach rumbled down the street and disappeared in a cloud of dust.

She went limp. All life seemed to drain out of her. The thought of the days ahead of her flashed through her mind in an endless stream of emptiness.

That night she stayed late at the paper. The small circle of light cast by the oil lamp at the edge of her desk was the only illumination in the dark office. She tried to concentrate on her work but found it difficult. Her mind kept veering off in tangents. She had felt the most devastating sense of loss. Lawrence was gone. A man who had become a best friend. A man who loved her and offered her everything most women would have been overjoyed to accept. Had she been wrong? Had she mistaken her leading? She thought she had made the right decision, but now the desolation of being alone to face whatever lay ahead swept over her in a paralyzing inertia.

She threw down her pencil, buried her head in her hands.

Just then she heard the rattle of the rusty doorknob of the newspaper door, followed by a loud, insistent banging. Mindy looked up startled. Some drunk probably wandered over from one of the saloons, having seen the light and stumbling up the steps. Should she ignore it or open the door and send whoever it was on his way?

Hesitantly, she got up from her desk. Just then the fierce knocking came again along with a familiar voice calling, "Mindy! It's me, Lawrence, please open up."

Lawrence! In a minute, Mindy rushed across the room and unlatched the door. A bedraggled, dusty, disheveled Lawrence stood there, grinning.

"What on earth!" she gasped. She had never seen Lawrence any way except immaculate, neatly dressed. "What happened to you?"

"A change of plans. At the first stage station, I got off the coach and hitched a ride back with a fellow hauling a load of lumber to Coarse Gold. Mindy, I hadn't gone but a few miles down the road when I knew I had to come back. I realized I didn't want to go back east. I didn't want to leave Coarse Gold. I didn't want to leave you."

He flung out both hands. "I realized I can't live without you. I don't want to live without you. Whatever we have to do, however we do it, I want to spend the rest of my life with you." He paused. "I love you, Mindy. More than I can tell you. More than I even knew."

Bewildered, Mindy wondered, *Could this really be happening?*

"Do I understand what you're saying, Lawrence? You want to stay here and help me with the *Gazette*?"

"If you'll have me." His eyes were full of hope. "I think I have some ideas that could help—" He stopped abruptly. "The important thing is, do you love me?"

She thought of the Biblical definition of love, especially the phrase, "Love does not seek its own." Instinctively she knew Lawrence's love for her was unselfish. He was proud of what she had accomplished, interested in her plans for the future. A future he was willing to share. The love he was offering was not binding but infinitely freeing. How she knew that, she wasn't sure, but she did.

"Do you, Mindy? You haven't said it yet."

Mindy felt confirmation rush up within her. She suddenly knew Lawrence was everything she had been searching for. In him she could imagine a life of shared dreams, goals, and mutual support. All that and a loving companionship besides. As he drew her slowly into his arms to kiss her, her lips were already forming the words. "Yes—"

EPILOGUE

Monday morning of the next week, Mindy walked into the back room where Pete was setting type. So much excitement and happiness was bubbling inside she wondered if it showed. She stopped beside him, waited until he had finished the line and shoved the stick into place. "Pete, you'll have to reset the paper's masthead."

The furrows in the printer's brow deepened as he raised his scraggly eyebrows. "What's wrong with it?"

"We have to change the editor and publisher's name."

"What do you mean? We just did that when you took over."

"I know but still there's a new name."

Pete's mouth dropped open, almost losing his teeth. "You sold the paper?"

"No, but this is the way the masthead should read from now on." She handed Pete a slip of paper. He glanced at her suspiciously then down at the paper. His lips moved as he read what she had written. He looked up again and growled, "Is this some kind of joke?"

Mindy thrust out her left hand, wiggling her third finger on which the new gold band shone. "That's my new name, Pete. Lawrence and I were married over the weekend."

"Is that a fact?" Pete grinned. "Well, I'll be . . . he's a fine fellow. Liked him right off. A lot like the boss, wouldn't you say?" He winked at Mindy, "I mean like Byron." Pete looked over his type faces, nodding his head. "Now let's see. This here will look nice set in Bedonia—don't you think? Independence Day, Editor."

Also from the
Westward Dreams Series

Bestselling author Jane Peart takes readers to the Old West in four novels of excitement, adventure, and romance. From mining camps to California vineyards, you'll meet women who must find new lives for themselves in a difficult, sometimes hostile environment. But with persistence, principle, and a steadfast faith, they not only survive, they thrive.

Runaway Heart: Book 1

Softcover 978-0-310-28802-2

Promise of the Valley: Book 2

Softcover 978-0-310-28800-8

Where Tomorrow Waits: Book 3

Softcover 978-0-310-28804-6

A Distant Dawn: Book 4

Softcover 978-0-310-28799-5

Pick up a copy today at your favorite bookstore!

Introducing the
Brides of Montclair Series

In this series of faith and love best-selling author Jane Peart traces the generations of the Montrose family of Virginia, starting before the Revolutionary War. To date, it is one of the longest-running historical-romance series on the market.

Courageous Bride
Softcover 978-0-310-20210-3

Daring Bride
Softcover 978-0-310-20209-7

Destiny's Bride
Softcover 978-0-310-67021-6

Folly's Bride
Softcover 978-0-310-66981-4

Fortune's Bride
Softcover 978-0-310-66971-5

Hero's Bride
Softcover 978-0-310-67141-1

Jubilee Bride
Softcover 978-0-310-67121-3

Mirror Bride
Softcover 978-0-310-67131-2

Ransomed Bride
Softcover 978-0-310-66961-6

Valiant Bride
Softcover 978-0-310-66951-7
Mass Market 978-0-310-66951-7

Yankee Bride
Softcover 978-0-310-66991-3

A Montclair Homecoming
Softcover 978-0-310-67161-9

Pick up a copy today at your favorite bookstore!

Share Your Thoughts

With the Author: Your comments will be forwarded to
the author when you send them to *zauthor@zondervan.com*.

With Zondervan: Submit your review of this book
by writing to *zreview@zondervan.com*.

Free Online Resources at
www.zondervan.com/hello

 Zondervan AuthorTracker: Be notified whenever your
favorite authors publish new books, go on tour, or post
an update about what's happening in their lives.

 Daily Bible Verses and Devotions: Enrich your life
with daily Bible verses or devotions that help you start
every morning focused on God.

 Free Email Publications: Sign up for newsletters on
fiction, Christian living, church ministry, parenting, and
more.

 Zondervan Bible Search: Find and compare
Bible passages in a variety of translations at
www.zondervanbiblesearch.com.

 Other Benefits: Register yourself to receive online
benefits like coupons and special offers, or to participate
in research.

ZONDERVAN®
.com